No Corpse

A Tally McGinnis Mystery

No Corpse

A Tally McGinnis Mystery

By

Nancy Sanra

RISING
TIDE
PRESS

Rising Tide Press
3831 N. Oracle Road
Tucson, AZ 85705
520-888-1140

Printed in the United States on acid-free paper.

Publisher's note:
All characters, places, and situations in this book are
fictitious, or used fictitiously, and any resemblance
to persons (living or dead) is purely coincidental.

Cover art by MacGraphics

First Printing: September 2000

Sanra, Nancy
No Corpse/Nancy Sanra

ISBN 1-883061-33-4

Library of Congress Control Number: 00 134971

About the Author

Nancy Sanra and her partner, Sherry, live in the Pioneer Valley at the foot of the beautiful Berkshire Mountains in western Massachusetts. Besides writing the Tally McGinnis mystery series, Nancy also writes children's books and has recently published two books in a series for children with special needs. A graduate of the University of California, she currently is holding creative writing seminars and classes. Along with actively participating in the local lesbian community, Nancy and Sherry enjoy hiking, golfing, swimming and an occasional glass of Amaretto with good friends. Nancy considers herself a pizza connoisseur and gladly invites anyone to drop by and share a slice of her famous pepperoni, sausage and black olive extravaganza. "Life doesn't get any better than a good pizza and new friends."

Nancy can be reached through Rising Tide Press, 3831 N. Oracle Rd. Tucson, AZ 85705 or www.risingtidepress.com.

FOR SHERRY

WHENEVER I LOOK AT YOU I JUST SMILE

ALSO BY NANCY SANRA...............

NO WITNESSES

NO ESCAPE

Available at www.risingtidepress.com or your favorite
bookstore.

Prologue

Friday, March 1, 1973
4:35 p.m.

Anna St. Amand stood on the bridge where the bay opened to the sea. Angry black clouds digested the lilac sunset. The air was crisp and cold. The two-lane highway that extended from Anacortes to Whidbey Island was deserted.

Her face was thin, her black eyes shifted with the mood of the moment. Bundled in a long, wool cape, Anna clutched a single razor blade in her fist. She squeezed her hand tightly feeling the blade cut deeply into her flesh. Blood seeped through the spaces between her fingers and dripped onto the black asphalt pavement.

Slowly and precisely Anna walked to the bridge railing. An instant's pause, and then she began to print her message. Blood red letters on cold gray steel. *Five blind mice with hearts of ice.*

She stood back and then carefully stuffed her driver's license and student I.D. between the bars of the bridge railing.

Anna paused, taking it all in: the black recess below, dozens of white and gray seagulls that rode the currents of wind, a boat with a throbbing red beacon bobbing in the distant waters.

Wiping the blood from her hand, Anna looked at her printed words. "Far better than a note," she said, thrilled with her bloody message. "They will suffer and they will pay." Her laughter was lost in the whirl of the Chinook winds. And then she shut out everything but what she meant to do.

Anna's eyes widened in terrible comprehension. Her crimson cape fluttered and snapped with the rush of air and for a split second the cape mushroomed into a hapless parachute.

The fishermen below watched the body make a slow, tumbling descent. Head flapping like a rag doll, arms flailing.

1

The Present
Saturday, July 11
3:35 p.m.

There was a cool summer breeze, but the sun was bright and reflected off the water through the curtains in their spacious stateroom.

Katie O'Neil pushed the buttons on the built-in mahogany stereo. Soon the room was filled with Mozart's "Flute Concerti."

She took three or four steps and smiled as if some private thought amused her. She surveyed the king-size bed and began taking off her clothes. First her "Olivia" T-shirt, then bra, then red shorts. She paused knowing Tally's eyes were on her and then Katie dropped her panties to the floor.

"I love you," Tally managed to whisper.

"Aye." Katie smiled with her eyes. "I promised myself, Tally McGinnis, if I ever got you away from San Francisco and the Phoenix Detective Agency, the first thing I'd do is remind you why the Irish are such happy folk." Her grin, both girlish and surprising, was filled with mischievous charm and flirtatious passion.

Seeing Katie's slim body before her, Tally nearly tripped over a suitcase on her way to the bed. Her eyes warmed. Then she felt the softness of Katie's hand tugging at her shirt. There was a quiet joy as she undressed and a quivering of her body as she brought her mouth to Katie's.

Part of Katie's personality, Tally had learned early on, was a deep appreciation of the gift of love and the view that passion should never be squandered.

The clean smell of Katie's skin was everywhere-the curly softness of her hair, the warmth of her slender hips. For a time, they lay in each other's arms, Tally holding Katie, her fingers slowly tracing her face, her nipples, the delicate curve of her back. Her broad pale lips were soft and warm as they explored Katie's neck.

Reaching up, shivering with urgent desire, Katie kissed Tally's eyes, the firm tips of her breasts. Her hand stroked wetness. Her hips rose in a desperate need to touch skin to skin.

After a time, this was not enough.

Tally allowed her eyes to memorize every inch of Katie's delicate frame as they began, with certain patience, to fulfill their need. Her mouth slid down Katie's stomach, and then they both were lost.

****

The crisp lines of Juvention Herrero's stiffly starched busboy uniform impressed him as he ran his shaky fingers down the lapel of his short-waisted, white jacket. He had never known such finery nor looked so handsome.

For three days, prior to boarding the beautiful cruise ship, sickness had taken his appetite and diarrhea had zapped most of his strength. Sometimes he had a fantasy his mother would return and care for him.

To rid his body of the illness, his manbo, the female, voodoo priest, had produced charms to honor the spirits. She had danced to a pulsating drumbeat at the small cult house and offered animal sacrifices at the altar in the jevo. First a chicken, then a goat. Blood was dripped across Juvention's distended stomach and the manbo provided a small vile filled with white powder to further relieve his symptoms. Juvention told no one else of his illness.

Sun leaked through the closed curtains casting shadows on the wall as he emptied the vile of white powder in a glass of water and raised it in a toast. His movements were mechanical as if planned or rehearsed many times. "Soon," he said in a deferred tone, "we will find Mother and I will be happy."

He quickly gulped down the contents. He was not about to be late his first afternoon on the job.

The pain in his stomach came back with sudden, new intensity, radiating from his bowels upward. He gasped for breath, betrayal in his eyes as he stared at the lone figure across the room. Along with the pain came a drenching sweat. He breathed in deeply. His image, in the mirror in his small crew cabin, wavered before his eyes and then darkness closed in. His body slumped to the floor without further movement. A few seconds later, his extra uniforms were removed from the closet and the door to his cabin softly closed.

****

The gentle sway of the curtains and low hum of the huge cruise ship engines, signaled to both Katie and Tally that their dream vacation had officially begun.

They lay in bed, their skin damp from lovemaking, a white rumpled sheet barely covering their naked bodies.

At thirty-eight, through no art of her own, Tally still looked deceptively youthful. She had never fully assessed her physical self and had no idea how attractive she was. There were barely any lines on her face. The complexion that had caused her to be carded for alcohol throughout her twenties served her well now. Her red-blond hair, cut in a short bob, was both silky and chic in appearance. She was a strong woman, opinionated and at times bossy, yet an inherent gentleness/vulnerability kept her from arrogance. She enjoyed having authority and wore it naturally.

Raised in a well-to-do section of San Francisco, her education was topnotch and her business sense beyond reproach. Tally's mind was quick and there was little she missed, either spoken or inferred. While she had once been a crack inspector for the San Francisco Police Department, she now oversaw a bustling private detective agency. Most of her assignments were routine domestic disputes and missing persons-the exception being her specialty, homicide investigation. She was a woman obsessed with her work and with her need to save humankind from its evil side. Days and evenings found her trying to juggle the ever-increasing workload and her personal life. But what struck Katie at the moment was the love she saw in Tally's deep emerald eyes.

Life held few surprises for Tally, but Katie's love-coming as it had after their years as business associates-had been as surprising as it was welcome. Tally had a keen awareness that happiness was fragile and love a gift that was often taken for granted. Katie had given her life a center and with that came the knowledge that all things seemed possible.

"What shall we do first?" Tally's voice was filled with anticipation as she stared deeply into Katie's lovely blue eyes, trying to decide if they were the color of the sky or deep azure water just outside their large bay window. Katie looked at her. The unencumbered sky, Tally decided, a depth of blue that went on forever.

Katie raised her head from the pillow, her shoulder-length brown hair framed her fair skin and delicately sculpted face. Raised in a poor family, she had a lively mind and, on occasion, a sharp tongue. "I think you mean second," she teased coyly in her soft Irish lilt.

Tally felt herself grinning. "Since I seem to be having some trouble with my numeration, maybe we should start over at the beginning."

"Aye," Katie whispered, "the very beginning," and then the telephone rang.

Tally sat up straight, attentive, startled.

"Let it go," Katie pleaded.

Playfully Tally smiled, her eyes flashing mischief. "Can't, ship could be sinking."

"'Tis indeed a possibility, Tally McGinnis, but I'd be doubting such a catastrophe could befall us when we've only just set sail a few hours ago on calm waters," Katie said with feigned indignation.

Katie was no stranger to the ocean. Born in Dublin, she had spent her summers helping her uncle on his less-than-seaworthy fishing boat. She knew the beauty and untamed power of the sea. And

Katie also knew Tally could never pass up a phone call for fear of missing something important.

Pulling the sheet down, Tally leaned over brushing her lips against the hollow of Katie's stomach. "It's probably just a steward checking to see if we need anything." She answered the phone on the fourth ring.

"Where the hell are you?" Cid Cameron's raspy voice needed no introduction.

Cid had recently retired from the San Francisco Police Department and, along with Tally and Katie, was now one-third owner of the Phoenix Detective Agency. With a fair amount of success they had tried to find a balance between their personalities and working styles.

Externally Cid was austere, but her heart was gold and her love for Tally and Katie never wavered.

Outside of police work, Cid had spent her life caring for her elderly mother. Mrs. Cameron had been a difficult, stern-faced woman who made it clear on a daily basis that she ruled the roost. She died seven years ago oblivious of the fact that her only child, Cidney, had sacrificed her happiness for a life of service to her.

"Ship set sail hours ago, for Christ sake." Cid continued, not waiting for a response from Tally. "Thought the two of you were going to meet me on deck. Embarkation party was a kick. Lots of pink rum drinks with fresh pineapple, cherries, and those damned little blue paper umbrella's that get stuck in your nostril every time you try to take a sip. And women, Tal, everywhere I look. Wonderful, beautiful women!"

Tally laughed aloud. Cid's call, Tally knew, was her way of checking to make sure both she and Katie were safe. A reflection of Cid's thirty-two years of working law enforcement, as well as Cid's way of announcing that she was in need of some help to break into the social scene-an area that she normally approached with extreme skepticism and fear. At fifty-four and overweight, Cid was more at home with a cold crime scene than she was with the prospect of a warm lover in a soft bed.

Tally looked at Katie and smiled. "Sorry we missed the party, we had a few things to tend to in our cabin."

"I bet," Cid teased. "First seating for dinner is in thirty minutes. That's us. We've been assigned a table for eight. Dress is casual. I'll pick you and Katie up in fifteen minutes…and Tal, we've got seven glorious days of island hopping in the Caribbean…don't you and Katie wear yourselves out the first night."

2

Saturday, July 11
5:45 p.m.

The Sea Pearl's main dinning room held 150 tables, each seating two to eight passengers at an early and late serving. The sidewalls were a series of windows that overlooked the deep aqua waters of the Caribbean Sea. The stately room was magnificent, a combination of crystal chandeliers, dark teak paneled walls and flowered, pink wallpaper in a rose pattern. The end wall, ahead of them, had built-in teak cabinets running the length of the room ending at the kitchen entrance and tasteful waist-high, carved railings discretely designated the waiter's assigned areas of responsibility. Several wide paintings depicting the sea in a palette of greens and blues brought the room to life and managed to convey an air of prosperous comfort.

The maitre d', a tall good-looking man with a shock of black hair, helped them to their seats and then politely bowed at the waist. "Enjoy your dinner," he said quickly hurrying away, the thick mauve carpet muffling his footsteps.

"Why," Cid asked not bothering to hide the irritation in her voice, "are we sitting at a table for eight instead of three?" The exact opposite of Tally's image, Cid was pulpy and rumpled. Her unruly thatch of gray hair was still damp from her shower and her signature navy Dockers and crisply starched white shirt were wrinkled from her hasty packing job. She gave the impression of not caring much about anything--that was a contrived deception. Cid had learned early in her career, as a beat cop, that she could learn more by not seeming to have authority and by concealing her keen intelligence.

"Bonding, dearie. Large tables are good for that sort of thing," said a smiling woman with exotic blue eye shadow and nearly white bleached hair. Her gaze was steady as she pulled a chair from the table and flopped her tall round body next to Cid. Her appearance was average, yet it was obvious she understood the subconscious visual effect of clothing and jewelry. She wore a smart, white, tropical worsted pantsuit and pale-blue blouse scooped low at the bodice, accented with a short strand of pearls.

"One of the cruise industry's mottos is mingle, merriment and re-book. They figure the more people we meet- the better the odds we'll have a good time and come back for future amusement. Not a bad plan when you think about it. New friendship and laughter is good for the soul," she continued extending her hand. "So are lesbian cruises. Mimi Wingate. Seattle, Washington. Computer programmer. Single and looking." Her smile became broader and more charming.

Long ago Tally had learned to trust her ability to make a rapid assessment. This was not a judgmental issue, just another former cop whose innate distrust of the human species necessitated conformation of another's goodness. Jobs, laughter and politics were just some of the things people wanted seen, but the duty of a good cop was to see the hidden agenda. Without appearing to watch her as closely as Tally did, she immediately sensed astute shrewdness from Mimi Wingate.

If Cid was intimidated, she didn't show it. She simply gave a what-the-hell-shrug and took Mimi's hand in hers. "Cidney Cameron. Cid. San Francisco. Retired cop. Private investigator now." She drew a breath and turned, "My business partners, Tally McGinnis and Katie O'Neil. Katie runs the office; Tally and I do the leg work."

Tally nodded and allowed herself to openly examine Mimi. She had a long face, high forehead and her makeup was thick, as if to hide the signs of advancing age. Her mouth was generous and seemed to promise smiles and kisses to anyone who captured her attention.

"Already in trouble with the law, eh, Mimi?" Marjorie Temple's voice was brittle and tinged with sarcasm. She walked to the far side of the round table tautly. She waited for her two companions to sit before folding her svelte frame into a chair.

"Mimi's always been our good-will ambassador. Good for a laugh. Good for a drink. Good for a cheap bleach job. Just good. Eh, Mimi?"

For a moment the tension silenced the table. Katie cast an astonished glance at Tally.

Then Mimi forced herself to smile. When she spoke, her tone was shamed. "College roommates," she said reining in her emotions, "a reunion of sorts." She looked at Cid and then dropped her eyes to the table.

Smoothly and with a flickering smile, Tally reached across the table and gave Mimi's arm a brief sisterly squeeze. "Laughter and merriment may be good for the soul, but I've always thought blondes were pretty damn special too."

Mimi remained silent. Faintly blushing with pleasure at the subtle rebuke directed at Marjorie.

Just to Marjorie Temple's left, an androgynous- appearing woman with clear blue eyes peering from a face decimated by old acne scars, slapped the table as if reprimanding a child. "That's just hunky-dory, Marjorie, you really know how to cast a shadow over a festive moment. At the very least try to pretend you can be pleasant. We're here for a good time. I'd have thought after all these years your sharp edges might have worn down some, or perhaps, you would have learned to put aside your petty jealousies and share the spotlight."

She looked at Katie first and then Cid and Tally. "I'm Cimarron Brooks." Her movements were quick and confident, her dark hair short and cut in a manly fashion. Her drawl had a southwestern twang and her clothes suggested comfort over style. Her large frame was carelessly covered in faded Levi's, a bright-yellow cowboy shirt and brown boots that were polished to a dull gloss.

"I apologize. Marjorie's always been a rip-snorter. Our prized bovine. Although she hates the comparison, there's no missin' the similarity. She bellows like a cow in heat and will trample anythin' in her path when food's close at hand, but it won't take you a heck of a lot of time to figure out she's more smoke than fire.

"For the good or bad of it, we are indeed old college roommates. University of Washington. And, although I know you'll find it hard to believe after listenin' to us bicker, we're family, and we all love each other."

Marjorie Temple leaned forward, her smile tight, her lips nearly white. She was pretty and even when she wasn't smiling; her dimples softened her face casting a certain levity to her harsh personality. "Shall the rest of us introduce ourselves or shall we continue with the *Old McDonald* farm comparisons?"

Marjorie seemed unnaturally still, her silk violet blouse clinging to her perfect round breasts. She was quite slender and her naturally blond hair barely touched her shoulders--not a strand out of place. Her mouth was generous and her snubbed nose was dotted with a few tiny freckles. She took obvious pleasure in her appearance.

"Marjorie Temple," she said, with an air of attentiveness and a style that reflected taste. "I'm the fashion editor for *Bon Ton* magazine and reside in Manhattan." She gave Cid a look of condescension. "That's New York City. And although I'm single, I'm certainly not interested in seeking the companionship of anyone aboard ship." Her arms didn't move, they elegantly danced as she spoke.

A Filipino waiter quietly filled their water glasses. Other waiters in starched white jackets, hurried between tables and the kitchen. The festive raucousness of voices filled the room.

"I'm Claire Taylor," a weak voice announced just to Katie's right. Claire's body was fragile and thin, her nose too pronounced for her tiny face. She looked like a soccer mom from the suburbs who rejected adornments and was a well-educated intellectual. "Mimi and I are the only ones to have remained in Washington after we completed college."

Tally and Katie smiled and nodded. Cid's head was angled toward Mimi Wingate. But Tally knew she wasn't missing a word that was being said.

"Bellingham, Washington, is my home town." Claire continued, pulling her soft white cardigan around her shoulders. Then she folded her hands in front of her as if in prayer. "I work as the city librarian and my partner Candice also works for the library. She was quite sad not to join me on this trip. In actuality, it's the first time we've been separated for any length of time since we committed ourselves to each other eighteen years ago."

"Here we go again," Marjorie interrupted, her voice suggesting careless disregard for those around her. "No phone conversation or occasion is complete without Claire slyly announcing that she among us is the only one to have sustained a lasting relationship. Actually, Claire dear, Candice is a whining wimp and hasn't a clue how to hustle another female or she would have been long gone from your boring servitude." The bluntness of the remark again silenced the table.

Marjorie Temple had a barely discernible foreign accent, Tally observed, and a soft femininity that suggested a pleasant disposition that wasn't there. Tally was quiet for the moment feeling the sadness of this woman and then changed the subject.

"Cimarron. I like the name. It's different. Is that a sobriquet or your given name?"

Moving forward in her chair, Cimarron rested her arms on the table. "My mama was a great fan of Edna Ferber. Ever read *Cimarron?*"

Tally laughed at this. "In high school. Don't remember it, at least not much. Knowing me I probably read the last two chapters and bluffed my way through the test."

"Mama desperately wanted one of her children to be an author. She'd read *Cimarron* just before I was born and I guess she figured if she named me after the book I just might turn out to be her writer."

"Never realizing the distinct possibility," Marjorie sarcastically added, her smile a leer, "that she'd end up with a rancher, a glorified farmer who thinks she's a cowboy. Can you imagine a ranch in New Mexico? Horses, scorpions and dirty little cows. And, of course, let's not forget the pigs and the stench. It all sounds exceedingly boring, and with pork and beef futures slipping daily, not very profitable, Cimarron. A bright academic gone to seed. Were you able to get the dirt out from under your nails? Or is that an homage to your labors?"

Cimarron studied Marjorie coldly. The unrefined rancher was suddenly replaced by an astute protector. "Better a few dirty nails than some cosmopolitan snob whose forgotten her roots and that it was her friends' generosity and smarts that got her through school and on the road to success. If my mind serves me well, Mikola Tetzlaffsky, you didn't even know how to hold a fork properly when you first arrived in this country from Russia and moved in with us. You go ahead and put on your airs for these nice folks here at our table, but be mindful of the degree of debt you owe your friends."

Cimarron's eyes narrowed slightly, further signaling her annoyance. "Karen Phelps tutored you all the way through school, sometimes going without sleep, and Claire Taylor taught you the necessary social niceties, includin' how to hold your fork and cut your meat. If it weren't for Mimi, you wouldn't have known the first thing about make-up or fashion. And least I forget poor Anna, if hadn't been for her doctorin' skills, you'd have been on the mommy track for the last twenty years instead of playin' Miss High Society."

Wide-eyed with astonishment, Marjorie sat frozen for a second and then flicked her wrist as if brushing away a pesky fly. "Drop the histrionics, Cimarron." Her face softened gradually and she focused on the one remaining vacant chair at the table. "I see Karen's late as usual."

"Karen will be here." Claire defended softly, smoothing her short-clipped brown hair. "When I saw her earlier, she couldn't wait for dinner. Perhaps she's had trouble locating her luggage or some such thing."

Cid gave Mimi a philosophical shrug. "Damn glad we're not sitting at a table for twelve, I don't think I could handle all the laughter and merriment."

Tally grinned, but her eyes were flat. This was hardly the romantic evening she had envisioned for their first night at sea. And, outside of a couple of interesting personalities, she certainly never would have picked this quarrelsome group as dinner companions.

She lifted Katie's hand and softly brushed her lips across the back. When Katie looked up, Tally winked and smiled. Katie had never seemed more beautiful. Her brown hair drawn back from her face, lips elegant and warm, her blue eyes laughing as if she were seeing everything for the first time.

Katie caught Tally staring and returned the wink, pressing Tally's arm close to her body. She was five years younger than Tally, but she brought understanding and insight to their relationship, harbored a love of beauty and laughed with a warmth that put everyone at ease. And, at night she wore short, pink nightgowns that drove Tally deliciously mad.

Looking directly at Tally, Claire rested her elbows on the white linen tablecloth and slid on oversized red glasses that dominated her face. "I hope you don't mind my curiosity, but goodness, your job does sound fascinating and so macho. Why did you choose to become a private detective?"

"In truth, I like my own game plan. Like to spend as much time as necessary on an investigation and I don't like a backlog of unsolved cases." Tally reflected now. Her ambitions had always been simple: Be a good cop, start a business, earn her father's pride.

With a mixture of awe and curiosity Claire asked, "Do you encounter violent physical contact when you're on a case? And are you proficient with a gun? I mean do you actually shoot people?"

Tally met the librarian's timid gaze with an amused smile. She wondered why the violent aspects of her career created the most inquisitiveness. It was not an easy job being a police officer or a detective, especially for a woman. Although the words, for the most part, remained unspoken, a woman cop is expected to be tough, but not offensive, a confidant and supportive partner, but not deferential, non-combative but ready without hesitation to defend and resolve any violent conflict. "We have our moments of confrontation, as does anyone in law enforcement. But certainly not to the degree television portrays. Still, there's always an element of danger in our line of work."

"I thought 'flatfoots,' that is what they call private detectives, isn't it?" Marjorie paused for effect, "were only glorified process servers."

Tally brushed back the fine ends of her coppery hair. Marjorie Temple was beginning to grate on her nerves.

"The field is large when it comes to detective work. Process serving is one aspect. We rarely—"

"Couldn't you be killed?" Claire pushed, her eyes fixed emphatically on Tally.

"That's a possibility, but I certainly hope not a probability," Tally answered with a lopsided grin, refraining from explaining the familiar entanglements of her job.

"Aye," Katie added proudly. She leaned sideways to touch her head against Tally's shoulder. "She can handle about anything that comes her way. She's well trained. Tally not only graduated from the police academy, but also has her degree in criminology and a black belt in karate. First-degree Shodan."

Tally's cheeks became pink with the spontaneous burst of adulation.

"Do you normally carry a gun? You know, pack a weapon in a holster and all?" Cimarron asked, obviously impressed.

Tally nodded. "One of the darker aspects of the job. A new Glock 40 caliber. I practice a couple of times a week at the police firing range and only carry a gun when I feel it's absolutely necessary."

"And I'll bet you belong to the NRA." Marjorie declared with authority, "and in your spare time shoot defenseless wild animals for sport and mount the trophies over your mantel."

Tally's wiry body straightened. She felt her stomach tighten into a fist. The petty part of her wanted to nail Marjorie for her short-sightedness, wish her an encounter with an armed stranger in a dark room and no law enforcement personnel with weapons to save her. But she knew better than to enter this word game with someone of Marjorie's sarcastic talents. She made do by saying mildly, "No, I don't belong to the NRA. And in fact, I'm an animal lover, domestic as well as wild. I favor the Brady bill or any other law that will take guns off the street and out of the hands of children and felons."

Cid turned, eyes flat and unfriendly. "I've never belonged to the NRA either, but I've met a few assholes that I wouldn't mind mounting over my mantel." She flushed, clearly angry as she openly glared at Marjorie Temple.

An uneasy silence settled over the table.

"And that's enough blather for now," Katie smiled a little, although her eyes did not. "Da used to say, 'Tis a poor man's fate, if he mixes work and play, for he ends up with diluted whiskey that leaves him neither drunk nor sober.'"

Tally felt the pressure of Katie's hand in hers and tried to smile.

From across the room a man in a black tuxedo eased up to their table. "Excuse me," he said his voice thick with a French accent. He had a silver chain around his neck. At one end of the chain, there was a medallion displaying the Shipmaster cruise logo. At the other end, a small sterling tasting cup. "I'm your wine steward for the duration of the cruise and I'm pleased to announce someone has ordered a magnum of Champagne for your table."

"Hot damn! That's the first coherent statement I've heard since I've been in the dining room." Cid slapped the table and grinned with pleasure. "Now, you back that Champagne with a double Glenlivet and you'll have made a friend for life."

Mimi touched Cid's hand. "Déjà vu. My drink of choice is Glenlivet." She looked at the wine steward. "Make that two and put it on my bill."

Gently, Katie prodded Tally. "'Tis love in bloom already."

Tally did not answer. She read Katie's comment for what it was: a joyful wish that Cid would find someone on this cruise to share her life. Someone to chase away the deep shadows of loneliness.

The wine steward flicked his right hand in the air and instantly a short, mustached busboy placed a huge iced container next to the table and then delivered the magnum of cold Champagne.

As the wine steward carefully peeled the gold foil seal from the cork, Marjorie said caustically, "Surely there's a card?"

"Forgive me." The wine steward produced a white envelope from the pocket of his jacket and laid it on the table.

Cimarron read the enclosed message aloud, the lines on her sun-baked face slowly turning into deep, dark furrows. "*And now there are but four blind mice with hearts of ice. Till we meet again, Anna.*"

Her mind reeling, Cimarron looked upward as if addressing a higher power and crossed herself. "Sweet Jesus!"

Claire jerked her head back and let out a shrill squeal.

Mimi's eyes prowled the table coming to rest on Marjorie. "Is this your idea of a sick joke?"

"For God's sake, Mimi," Marjorie's glance was filled with disapproval and dislike. "I may have my faults, but I certainly don't use the dead to elevate my sense of adventure. Cheap theatrics, that's all. Anna's very dead and has been for over nearly thirty years. Remember, half a dozen people witnessed her death. This is probably one of Karen's practical jokes."

"Then why the reference to four blind mice?" Claire asked, her voice quivering. "And where is Karen?"

3

Saturday, July 11
7:15 p.m.

They took in the view together. The fading sun becoming a pool of orange in the distant Caribbean waters. The air was fresh and the sea still, save for the white foam that bubbled up from the back of the ship as it smoothly cut its wide path. The world left behind barely seemed to exist.

Tally had agreed to accompany Cimarron on her search for Karen Phelps after a frenzied grimness overtook the evening and made dining nearly impossible.

They had chosen the fresh air and steps over the elevator. Now both of them regretted the decision. Tally's green Izod shirt felt like a very large moistened stamp against her skin. It had been three flights down to the purser's office to find out Karen's cabin number, and six flights up to the Blue View Deck where her suite was located.

Cimarron's yellow shirt had a crease of dampness running the length of her back and her weighty boots thumped the deck as they walked. "Karen has made it her personal practice to be late for everythin'. And the Champagne, well hell, I'm just sure, despite what she says, that it was some of Marjorie's buffoonery. No-sir-ree-bob, Anna's dead." Cimarron slammed her fist into her palm. "God rest her soul, she's dead."

Tally couldn't help but notice the uncertainty in Cimarron's voice. And, at this point, her own curiosity was peaked. *Who was Anna and why did this quarrelsome group of former college roommate's think, or was it hope, that Anna was dead?*

For privacy reasons and to insure quiet from cheery travelers on the lower decks, the pricey Blue View suites were located on the top of the ship above the bow, with only the radio and supply room close by. The walls were dark inlaid mahogany. The carpet was a rich, royal blue. The scent of fresh-cut flowers was everywhere, and, for Tally, the word luxury seemed inadequate to describe the lush surroundings.

As they drifted down the hall, Tally immediately sensed something was wrong.

There was a flurry of activity, yet it was subdued. In fact, it was eerily quiet. Three room stewards stood with their backs stiffly pressed against the wall, ill at ease—as if they were about to bolt.

The captain, in his smart white uniform with gold and black braid, stood, shoulders slumped, talking in a whisper to a short bald man with olive skin and a beer belly that hung over his blue jeans. The intimacy of their conversation suggested to Tally that the bald man was also a member of the crew.

The suite numbers were posted on the doors. Odd numbers on one side of the hall, even on the other. It took Tally only a second to calculate that the somber crowd was standing in front of suite seventeen, Karen Phelps' room.

Cimarron must have computed the numbers as well. "What the hell's happened?" she demanded loudly, her broad face tense.

The captain turned. At first startled, he immediately regained his composer. Blocking Cimarron's forward motion with extended arms, he said in a heavily accented voice, "I must apologize. This area is temporarily off-limits."

In her middle to late forties, Cimarron was sturdily built with strong arms and well-calloused hands from years of fence mending and tending to her cattle. She abruptly pushed past the captain as if he were a mere shadow. Instinctively, Tally followed, only to stop short, just behind Cimarron, at the entrance to the suite. A nude body lay on the floor. A thin purple, bloody line ringed the dead woman's neck and a small trickle of blood ran down her chest stopping just short of her right breast.

Cimarron swayed, the doorframe catching her weight and keeping her from falling. "Oh, God!" The sight etched its impression into her brain until she felt her head ready to explode. Her legs buckled.

The bald man jerked his head, motioning for the captain to escort Cimarron away, and then he immediately shut the suite door, but not before Tally noticed a rather small hangman's noose lying next to the body.

"Your suite is near here, Signorina?"

Tally's face was taut when she focused on the short man standing in front of her. "No," she answered in a strained voice. She felt a sense of dread and the thrill of her romantic vacation evaporate as she reached in the back pocket of her crisply pressed khaki slacks for her detective I.D.

His face was round with suspicious black eyes that grew amused as he examined Tally's identification and handed it back.

"An American private detective." Tally noted his heavy Italian accent and the painstaking care he took to make sure his English was correct.

"These are international waters, but, I suspect, Signorina, you already know your license does not extend beyond the border of California. Si?"

"Vacation," Tally said raising her arms in mock surrender. She looked from one grim face to the other. Cimarron was pale and leaning heavily on the captain. Tally turned back and gazed at the bald man. "And you are?"

"Vincenzo Pallino, chief of security for Shipmaster Cruises." He sounded weary, but extended his hand and smiled. "You're from San Francisco. I've been there many times. A beautiful city and far more enchanting than even my lovely Milan."

Tally nodded as she shook his hand. She judged his age to be somewhere in his middle forties.

"And your business here on the Blue View Deck?" he asked, his eyes now clear and cold.

Tally gave a small shake of the head, more to herself than Vincenzo Pallino. Another second's pause and then Tally explained how she, along with Cid and Katie, had been drawn into their tablemate's web of petty envy, resentment and the search for a missing companion.

Room stewards, unnerved and scared, shuffled down the hall and out of sight. Tally was vaguely aware of the movement behind her, but her attention was riveted on the door in front of her. A dozen questions zipped through her well-organized mind. "Karen Phelps? I don't think my eyes deceived me, did they Mr. Pallino? Murder is what you're dealing with here, correct?" she asked, her face expressionless.

Hand raised, he cautiously yanked upward as if simulating a hanging. "An unfortunate death, probable suicide," Vincenzo's tone was controlled, careful. "Our guests pay many lira for fun and entertainment. To suggest or so much as hint that this unfortunate mishap were murder could not only spell disaster for the cruise line, but would create an atmosphere of fear. Our passengers left their troubles behind at embarkation. Murder is something that happens back home in the big cities, not while on a luxury liner in the Caribbean. Capisce?"

The bluntness of Vincenzo Pallino's suicide scenario, combined with his dissuasiveness struck Tally as strange and sent caution straight to her gut. "Surely you're not suggesting the hangman's noose I just saw is responsible for Karen Phelps' death?"

His black eyes never wavered as he nodded solemnly.

Tally read his expression for what it was: a bald lie.
She tapped the toe of her thin-soled loafer against the carpet. "So," she said with intensity, stepping toward Karen Phelps' suite, "a woman dies, and for seven days you sweep the whole matter under the carpet. Call it suicide? Is that a cruise ship credo or your clever way of dealing with the curious?"

Considering his bulk, Vincenzo Pallino moved with agility, nervously blocking her path. His mouth tightened. "You're wrong, Signorina," he said with a sour smile. He looked over Tally's shoulder, praying no one else would hear or see the commotion. His eyes locked on the captain's and then his big hands gently pulled Tally to the side.

"Suicide or murder is not a usual occurrence on a cruise. Drunk and disorderly. Perhaps petty theft. Once, as you American's say, in a blue moon, a sexual assault. We have had passengers die of heart attacks or strokes, but never murder."

She tilted her head considering him. She felt like she was being leaned on, led down the garden path. "Sounds like you're caught in political cross fire. The cruise lines like to keep a squeaky-clean image. Still, murder is murder. This woman had family and friends. Sooner or later someone will have to be held accountable for her death. If you are exceedingly cleaver, Mr. Pallino, you may be able to momentarily convince the dead woman's traveling companions that she died as a result of suicide."

Pausing, Tally glanced at Cimarron. "Recently, in the United States, there was mass media coverage on the attempts of the cruise industry to minimize crimes committed against passengers. You may be part of that conspiracy. Whether you're aware of it or not, I don't know, but I'm afraid my business partner, Cid, and I spent too many years working homicide in San Francisco to buy a scenario that suggests the body I briefly saw was anything less than murder. The noose was small, probably not capable of bearing weight. There was blood on Karen Phelps' neck and her face was bluish purple, all of which could be attributed to hanging, but I'd guess strangulation. In a hanging, the rope slips, leaving two marks...I only saw one."

A look of recognition registered for a second and then for the first time Vincenzo Pallino looked impatient. His voice went cold. "Your powers of observation are commendable, but maybe not as reliable as you would wish."

He gave a brief sardonic smile. Tally thought she saw a sudden flare in his dark eyes. "This could have happened before embarkation. Assuming, as you do, that there is a crime here, the perpetrator may not even be on board. Think of the panic, Signorina, if I do not handle this with the utmost discretion. I take my position seriously and I would be a less than creditable employee if I allowed you to continue to believe that Shipmaster Cruises, or the cruise industry in general, would use their bottom line as motive to allow a crime to be swept under the carpet."

Vincenzo Pallino hooked his thumbs over the corner of his pants pockets and scanned the hall. "There are 1200 passengers on board and 900 crew. To undertake the investigation and interrogation of such a large number would strain the resources of even the San Francisco police department." His dark hands seemed restless and, when he glanced at his watch, his left eyebrow twitched nervously.

"My staff is small. Two mediocre security guards as my only backup. My talents are sizeable," he continued with a playful grin, "but even I would find such a task daunting. I have notified my superiors and, as always, we will follow proper protocol. When we arrive at our next port of call the local authorities will have jurisdiction. Until I am told otherwise, the death of Signorina Phelps will remain listed as a suicide."

If Tally's experience was any guide, Vincenzo Pallino was a better politician than cop. But his eyes were bright and he was sophisticated in a savvy way.

"So when do we dock?" Tally asked, with more curiosity than demand. She had learned long ago it was better to have other cops as allies rather than opponents. Cultivating friendships meant access to information that wasn't normally available to just anyone.

Vincenzo's face was a road map of stress lines and sags. He raised his hands to his lips and steepled his fingers. A fine line of perspiration rested just above his pencil-thin black mustache. When he finally spoke, the dark lines beneath his eyes seemed to deepen. "If we maintain a normal course we would dock late tomorrow in St. Croix."

He hesitated a moment as if he were thinking quickly. "I may need some help preserving the death scene, Signorina, photographs— trace evidence. Perhaps even an opinion." His smile was a concession. "Already room stewards and the captain have disturbed the scene. You've dealt with this kind of case before. You have a frame of reference. Of course I'd have to check your credentials."

With an expression of melancholy, Tally brushed the ends of her strawberry hair back. She had little tolerance for mediocrity and knew the crime scene was already badly contaminated. "It seems to me, if I were to work for you I would be bound by Shipmaster Cruises' code of ethics and I'm not sure that standard meets mine. Besides, collecting trace evidence or taking photos is the job of a good forensics team. I have friends waiting in the dining room."

"Of course. Of course. Your business associates?"

Tally nodded.

Again Vincenzo waved his hand. "Earlier, Signorina, you mentioned your partner's name was Cid. That wouldn't be Lieutenant Cid Cameron by chance?"

"Why yes." Tally's voice reveled her astonishment. "She's retired now, but you know her?"

His smile was quizzical. "Six years ago I had the honor of spending three months in your fine city working the homicide division at the grand Hall of Justice. A little brush-up course for the Milan di Polizia, my former employer. I have fond memories of Cidney. A keen mind. Brilliant detective. And such an appetite for Chianti." His smile was cheerfully filled with joy. "Decies repetita placebit. When ten times repeated it will still please. I look forward to seeing her again."

Tally surveyed this short, round man with the gaudy St. Thomas tee shirt and plastic deck sandals. Her mouth parted as she realized who he was. She saw in his face, the kind friend Cid had once spoken of so often. "You're Vinny." She smiled, nearly laughed. "Cid's Italian friend, Vinny. Small world."

He winced. "Just call me Vincenzo." His smile vanished when he saw the captain looking his way. "This is not a good moment for joyful conversation. Perhaps, if you and Cidney were to join me in my office on the Bedeck?"

She glanced over her shoulder. "And Cimarron?"

"For now let her go back to her friends." There was defeat in Vincenzo's voice. "Even if I suggested discretion, she has the right to mourn this selfish, tragic act, as do her amico intimo. Her friends. Interrogation will come later when we know more about this tragedy."

The library occupied a small area just outside the dining room, with floor-to-ceiling shelves stocked with books, cozy leather chairs and an immense compass at the window. Standing just inside the door, Tally made herself imagine what Cid or Katie's death would do to her. She couldn't get to the feeling, but it pained her as she watched Cimarron haltingly talk.

Comprehension was slow in coming for the group of old college roommates as they learned of Karen Phelps' death.

"But how?" she heard Mimi Wingate ask, her lips barely moving. "Karen was happy, she'd never hurt herself, never hurt anyone...except maybe Anna." Her face went white as snow.

"Jesus," Cid whispered studying Mimi with open sorrow. She reached for her cigarettes and at the same time saw the "No Smoking" sign. With considerable irritation, she stuffed her Virginia Slims in the breast pocket of her white shirt and scuffed the carpet with the sole of her black orthopedic shoes. Her pants were a little too long and dipped low at the back catching on her heel. "Dammit, Tal, this is vacation, let Vinny do his job! Murder, suicide. Who the hell cares? Just because we're ex-cops doesn't mean we have a sign hanging around our necks offering free investigative skills."

The solemn expression on her pugnacious features softened as she looked sympathetically at Mimi. "She needs me. I mean I'm anxious, even excited to see Vinny, but Tal, Mimi's lit a fire in me. We talked while you were gone. She knows everything about me, and thinks I'm super I might add. I haven't felt like this in fifteen years." She puffed out her chest and hiked up her pants exposing socks that didn't match. "Maybe since I was in my twenties."

Tally's gaze combined surprise with caution.

"I know, I know, I just met her." Cid shrugged, her hands now in the pockets of her pants. "Hell, she really likes me, wants to walk in the moonlight tonight. God only knows where that will lead." Her laugh was nearly a giggle. "I'm not saying it's love, not this soon...but, Tal, it's my one shot at love in years. Murders' been my whole life for longer than I care to remember. I'm ready for something new, something wonderful. I'm not the first person to have a shipboard romance. Who knows, by the end of the cruise it may be kaput, but for now it feels wonderful. As long as my back ain't got a target on it, count me out. This is Vinny's turf and Vinny's scumbag to catch. And what about Katie, Tal? This is her vacation too."

As Tally turned and looked at Katie she felt her own vulnerability. Tense, Tally saw the hesitance in Katie's eyes, the disappointment, as well as the professional understanding that normally made complaint impossible.

Katie's tone, as so often, combined a hint of joy along with seriousness. "We're two people in love who have never been away together. This is our time."

Tally knew if she had any sense she would cut and run --forget what she saw in Phelps' suite. Forget Vincenzo Pallino. After all, no matter how carefully camouflaged, a cover-up by Shipmaster cruises had already been neatly laid out for her. The stench from this little scenario made her want to vomit. For a moment Tally's green eyes held the coolness of loathing. Then she thought of the dead woman and knew immediately she had to go back, had to find out what really happened in suite seventeen.

The case. Always, always, always the case.

Cupping Katie's face in her hands, Tally lightly touched her lips to Katie's forehead. "I won't be long." She kissed her as much out of need as to thank her for her understanding.

"You're stubborn like your father, Tally McGinnis," Katie said with quiet intensity, looping her arm through Tally's.

Mentally Tally winced. She felt herself stiffen. Patrick McGinnis had loved her, showered her with as much attention as his career aspirations would allow. But he had been the district attorney, he belonged to the people, and his job came first. Even affection for Tally's mother had been set aside while in search of the next big case. The next big trial. Tally gazed at Katie with the look of uncomfortable discovery.

Unexpectedly Katie leaned forward, her head resting on Tally's shoulder. She seemed to gauge Tally's strength of will. "Go," she said finally with an ambiguous smile, "but I'll have you remember, there's a wee commitment ceremony tomorrow morning at ten. It's very important to me."

"I wouldn't miss it." And then, the wonder of her good fortune made Tally smile. "Am I really stubborn?"

Katie pulled back, mildly amused. "Without a doubt."

"Stubborn? Shit!" Cid made a sour face.

"Hush, Cidney Cameron," Katie gave a theatrical sigh, "you're both cut from the same loaf of bread." Her face was thoughtful, and then she smiled, "I'd be bettin' you'll accompany Tally."

Turning and looking at Tally, Cid felt the weight of a possible crime, knew the expectations. She gave half a shrug. "Just tell Mimi I'll catch up with her later, we'll have a drink and then take that moonlight stroll."

4

Saturday, July 11
8:55 p.m.

Unlike any other crime scene, the area had not been cordoned off. Vincenzo Pallino unlocked the faux mahogany door, nervously waiting for a group of women returning from dinner to pass, before allowing Cid and Tally to enter Karen Phelps' suite. He scanned the hall again before entering himself.

There was enough evening sun left to make the room somewhat bright. The air of merriment that had accompanied the joyous reunion between Cid and Vincenzo was coldly forgotten when glazed dead eyes greeted their arrival.

The pungent smell of death was everywhere and for a second Tally wanted to dash downstairs where the fanfare of laughter was all that mattered and murder was found in a book in the ship's library. But the deed of an evil intruder had already left its mark on her mind and she knew, regardless of where she went, the image of Karen Phelps' lifeless body could not be erased until her death was resolved. In a small notebook she made a quick sketch of the room, along with the body position.

Wide windows opened to a pricey view of endless sea. The suite was large with each area flowing into the next. Living room, bedroom, outside patio. A nondescript mahogany cabinet in the corner contained a TV, VCR and compact disk player. The addition of several flower arrangements along with four nice watercolors created an atmosphere of quiet opulence as well as cordial comfort.

Cid carefully stepped across the body that lay just inside the door and flicked on the light. For a moment they all seemed unnaturally still.

Excluding her neck wound, Karen Phelps looked perfectly healthy-a Matisse nude posed on a sea of blue carpet. Well-coifed auburn hair, shapely petite body, beautiful face.

"Christ, must be a hundred degrees in here." Cid gave a grimace. "My cabin is cool, almost cold." She looked to Tally for conformation.

Nodding, Tally checked the thermostat. "Ninety-nine. Maybe Phelps had just showered and wanted it warmer. That would account for her nudity."

"The noose, Signorina Tally. A shower is an odd need prior to suicide." Vincenzo stopped as if at another thought. "Heat is also odd on a Caribbean cruise." He reflexively held his hand to his nose.

Tally shot a dagger look at the chief of security and then stood, hands on her hips, looking at the ceiling. "As I said earlier, the noose is too small. Besides, there's no place to attach a rope. Can't hang yourself in thin air." Her gaze moved to the body and she felt herself go cold. After all the dead bodies she had seen, she still had not hardened to the sight of one-still never forgot a victim's face.

"Noose is ornamental." Cid injected with authority. "Maybe the killer's marker. Certainly not a weapon for suicide." She hesitated and then shook her head, "But you knew that didn't you, Vinny?"

The moment of truth had come. Vincenzo spread his hands, but said nothing. For Cid, his gesture was silent affirmation.

Tally made herself smile, but eyed Vincenzo Pallino more closely as if ripping away his outer covering to see what really lay beneath the fabricated persona he had presented to her earlier.

Cid thoughtfully scratched her cheek. "What the hell do you do with a dead body on board ship. Still don't dump 'em overboard, do they Vinny?"

He laughed, a rumbling sound that made his ample belly jump. "As I told Signorina Tally, on occasion we have a heart attack or stroke victim. I have a small walk-in cooler next to the jail downstairs."

"Cooler and jail, huh. Who'd a thunk it? I'm impressed, Vinny."

Tally ignored the friendly banter and moved on to the expansive bathroom. White towels fell neatly from silver racks and small bottles of complimentary shampoo and lotion lined the counter top. A comb and brush lay next to the sink; the shower was clean and dry.

"If the victim hadn't showered," Tally asked to no one in particular as she exited the bath, "and it appears that's the case, doesn't it seem odd that she was nude? I mean there's no sign of forced entry, so either modesty wasn't an issue or she knew her killer intimately."

Restless and waving his hands for emphasis, Vincenzo answered, "Perhaps it was, how you say, a *surprise* attack?"

Cid jammed a cigarette in her mouth and quickly lit it. White smoke hung in the oppressive heat. "Like Tally said, no sign of forced entry. And the room is undisturbed. No fight. Her purse is sitting in plain view. This was no smash and grab. Hell, other than a coupla bloody heels," she pointed at Karen Phelps' feet, "from being dragged across the carpet, there's no sign of a struggle."

"Perhaps you are correct," Vincenzo said his voice revealing his unwillingness to let go of his theory. "You may recall when you first boarded ship your cabin door was open and your keys awaited you inside. The suites are no different. An intruder could easily have slipped into Signorina Phelps' suite and surprised her."

Cid rolled her eyes. "Right Vinny, and the list of suspects have now been narrowed to 10,000." Ability wise, Cid knew Vincenzo Pallino was a good administrator, but he was not a good cop. He lacked instinct.

Tally walked the length of the room and stopped next to the well stocked bar, a handsome teak cabinet that contained a small sink, refrigerator, liquor and soft drinks. A gift basket with blocks of cheese and a bottle of 1970 Chateau Lafitte Rothschild sat on the counter. Tally's eye's widened for a moment, then she turned to face Vincenzo.

"I agree with Cid. Where would someone hide?" She moved to a large closet, opened the door and took a laundry bag down from a hook checking the contents.

"For a few moments an intruder could hide beside the bed or in the closet or shower. But Karen Phelps wasn't in her room for just a few minutes. Her suitcases are unpacked and clothes hung up. Even the clothes she wore to board the ship have been put in this laundry bag. A surprise attacker wouldn't wait that long and chance discovery. I think we're dealing with someone she knew. One cool calculating customer." She let the laundry bag drop to the closet floor.

Vincenzo conceded with his hands and a shrug of his shoulders.

Tally stepped down into a small alcove that contained a queen-size bed covered with a colorful bed spread. Nearby, a nightstand held a lamp, book, reading glasses and a small picture of Cimarron Brooks and Mimi Wingate. A sign in the background announced: Welcome to Expo 2000 Tally stood silent, feeling the loss, gazing across the room at Karen Phelps, knowing death by strangulation takes several desperate excruciating minutes. Her voice was dry when she finally spoke. "Do we know if Phelps was traveling alone?"

Vincenzo lowered the thermostat and flicked on the air conditioning. He wiped his flushed face with his hand. "Si, as were all her friends. However, Signorina Phelps was the only one to have upgraded to a suite. Her immigration card listed her hometown as Milwaukee, Wisconsin, and her occupation as a physician and surgeon. How you say, gynecologist?"

"A woman's doctor," Tally elaborated. "Obstetrics, infertility, maybe some general care."

Vincenzo took an aggressive step forward. "Perhaps abortions?"

Tally shrugged. "The specialty is right, so it's certainly a possibility, but if you're thinking this is the work of some radical right-wing group, you're wrong. The more militant pro-lifers target abortion doctors all right, but with bombs and bullets. Did you run Phelps, see if she has a sheet? Or can you do that sort of thing from a ship?"

Vincenzo's mustache twitched. "Si. My computer, scanner and printer, how you say, are top-of-the-line." He qualified, "Her record is clean. No arrests. And her travel companions are also clean."

Careful not to disturb the field of evidence, Cid got down on all fours to examine the strangle wound more closely. To allow herself more freedom of movement she tugged on her shirt until one white tail hung loosely around her waist.

"Perp was strong," she said nonchalantly. "Probably used a thin ligature or wire of some kind. Wound is deep." She touched her own throat, as lifeless blue eyes seemed to follow her movement. "At some point Phelps' hands were bound too. Have a look Vinny."

He nodded and glanced at the barely visible purple contusions ringing Karen Phelps' wrists.

"And," Cid leaned over until her chin was nearly touching the carpet, "looks like the perp took a souvenir."

Tally's face froze in surprise.

"Patch of skin is missing from the right side of her butt. Fancy little star." Cid watched her words register in Tally's eyes.

"Bite-mark eradication?" Tally asked looking for offender traits. She stepped forward and stared at the wound that was mostly hidden by body position.

"Nope. This is Picasso with a knife."

"Perhaps," Vincenzo began and then his poker face fell silent.

It was somehow touching, Tally thought, to watch Vincenzo Pallino realize shipboard police work was more complicated than he had thought, and more dangerous than he had expected.

On a leather chair in the corner, across from the bed, clothes were neatly laid out: a pair of red cotton slacks, a red flowered short-sleeved shirt, skimpy white bikini panties and a single knee high. A beige bra, Tally noticed, was lying at the foot of the bed on the floor.

Tally's eyebrow arched, a nonverbal sign that anger was bubbling deep within her. "She was standing here," she said reconstructing, her green eyes fixed on the knee high. "Probably just starting to dress. I'd guess her back was to her attacker."

"And the perp nailed her while she wasn't looking," Cid added, still on all fours. "Maybe cold-cocked her. Bound her wrists and then the son of a bitch strangled her to keep her quiet."

"Close," Tally said, her expression haunted. "I'd bet she was gagged before she was strangled. And I'd also bet when she's autopsied the pathologist will find a tan knee high in her mouth or throat."

Vincenzo nervously wiped his forehead with a wrinkled handkerchief. "Perhaps she was dressing for the embarkation party and the killer boarded and disembarked just before we set sail."

"You may be right to a certain extent," Tally conceded with a razor's edge in her voice. "She surely was killed early on. I'm not a forensic pathologist, but this putrid smell suggests Phelps has been dead for a while. The high temperature in the room would not only accelerate decomposition, but intensify the odor and make identification of the exact time of death difficult. I believe she was killed shortly after we sailed, not before."

She pointed to a glass plate containing a half-eaten pickle and crust of wheat bread sitting on the corner of the bed. "I'd bet the cost of a cruise ticket that plate came from room service, and, if my mind serves me well, the brochure in my cabin stated there was no room service until after we set sail."

Vincenzo's surprised expression said he'd missed the plate when he had been in the room earlier. His gaze continued to sweep counter tops as he snatched a small phone from his belt and punched up three numbers. His call was lengthy; his voice muted by embarrassment. Only after he announced, "Scusa, scusa," to Cid and Tally, did he regain both his confidence and composer.

"It happens, Vinny, we all miss clues the first go around." Cid said, a plain-speaking comment she knew to be all too true.

Vincenzo replaced the phone on his belt. "We sailed promptly at 3:45. According to kitchen records, a ham sandwich with lettuce and tomato only was delivered to suite seventeen at 4:10."

"Any description of who answered the door?" Tally asked from across the room, realizing this investigation had already been so poorly handled that the chances of catching the killer were near zero.

"No, Signorina. The waiter, he saw only the $5.00 tip."

Using a pen from her breast pocket, Cid pointed to a red ribbon resting on Karen Phelps' leg. The initials, C.T. were neatly stitched in the shinny fabric. "What'd you make of this?"

"Just a bookmark," Vincenzo said with renewed authority.

"And pizza dough I don't have for a brain," Cid snapped, as she struggled to her feet and massaged the small of her back. "What the hell is a bookmark doing neatly lying across a dead woman's thigh? And whose initials are C.T.?"

Tally picked up the book from the nightstand. "*Emerald City Blues*," she read opening the cover. "'For my dearest Karen, A little reading material to remind you of our city. It's so good to see you again. Sharing the tranquil moments of this cruise are made special because you are here. Love and more love, Claire.'" Tally closed the book. "Maybe our little librarian isn't as devoted to her lover, Candice, as she led us to believe." She pointed to the bookmark. "C.T.? Claire Taylor."

"So, the skinny little runt iced her old college roommate?" Cid asked more as a challenge than a question. Crossing to the bar she searched the double-shot bottles for Glenlivet, settling for Cutty Sark.

Tally kept her voice even, a friend reasoning. "Doesn't fit. Claire Taylor is what, five feet tall if she's lucky. Underweight, as you so eloquently stated, and as fragile as a saltine cracker. That hardly fits the description of a killer capable of dragging and strangling Karen Phelps. It's obvious our murderer wanted the spotlight on Claire Taylor, the question is why?"

Cid drained the tiny bottle of Cutty Sark, waited for the warmth to hit her stomach and slid the empty in her pocket. "Who found the body, Vinny?"

"Room steward delivering fruit and mints. Patrons of Blue View suites are privileged. Although it is the aim of Shipmaster Cruises to make all of its guests feel pampered, the smallest of details are never forgotten here. A steward is always close at hand. Capisce?"

"Capisce, ca-crap, Vinny," Cid pushed her cigarette in her mouth with more force than necessary. "I got a hot date waiting downstairs. Gimme the facts not the bullshit. I wanta know if he saw anyone coming or going from this suite before or just after we set sail."

From the corner of Tally's eye she saw Vincenzo blanch. Watching him closely, she read a combination of both resentment and dependence. "You have interrogated him?" she asked.

"Si. The wine," he pointed at the gift basket, "was delivered by an attendant from the ship's liquor store, the duty-free shop. Also, the steward saw a woman."

Vincenzo's shiny dome revealed a small amount of perspiration. He looked first to Cid, a forgiving glance, and then to Tally.

"Big," he finally said, holding his two hands in front of his chest, his fingers spread wide. "Mama Pallino. How you say? Buxom?"

"Large breasts?" Tally asked.

"Si. Tall. Little too much pasta around the middle and very blond."

Keeping her voice mild, Tally said, "Mimi Wingate."

Cid eyed them both warily, feeling vulnerable and afraid. She tossed her cigarette in the sink next to the bar. "Back off, Tal. I don't like your implication. Being at Karen Phelps' suite doesn't make Mimi guilty of murder," she quickly defended.

"Un Momento." Vincenzo's tone was firm but gentle. A reclaiming of his rank as chief of security. He crossed to the opposite side of the room. Beneath a curtained window overlooking the small patio was a desk. He pointed to a brown blotter trimmed in matching leather.

"I found this earlier when I first looked for a suicide letter." A note, written on Shipmaster stationary was tucked neatly in the corner.

Cid and Tally stepped closer, bumping into each other as they reached the desk.

"I need to see you. Please don't put me off. The others must not know."

For a moment, Tally looked out the window, toyed with the gold chain she wore around her neck. "Mimi," she again softly repeated.

"Since when did you become a handwriting expert?" Cid asked harshly. She lit another cigarette and sucked in a long drag. She was steadying herself. Tally's professional skepticism was creating a distance between them that Cid had never intended to be there.

"Could be that dirtbag Marjorie!" she corrected with a defensive glare. "I repeat, being at Karen Phelps' suite doesn't make Mimi or anyone for that matter, guilty of murder."

Tally looked away. Her compassion real. "No, you're right. But it does make for an interesting interrogation. And don't forget you just met Mimi, you don't know anything about her."

"What's there to know? You're bringing your own biases to the table, Tal. That's not fair. At my age new friendship, maybe love, is both an instinct and a blessing. Mark my word, Mimi's good people. When the police get here, it'll be the Temple bitch they zero in on, not Mimi."

Tally's eyes flashed at her. "We already know Mimi had opportunity. For God's sake, Cid, Phelps was nude, maybe they were lovers and quarreled. That could constitute motive. You taught me the first rule in a murder investigation is never trust anyone. Don't tell me your cop antenna isn't vibrating just a little."

Cid's blue eyes paled under her gray bushy eyebrows as she tried to detach herself, suppress her apprehension. Her thoughts were interrupted by a knock on the door.

Vincenzo quickly answered, allowing only a few inches of space for whispered conversation. The exchange was brief.

"So to your knowledge," Tally asked when he returned, "the steward did not see anyone else in or around this suite besides the woman you described?"

Glancing at Cid, Vincenzo regarded her with distress and a measure of sensitivity that was so tangible Tally could feel it herself. He spread his hands in an apology. "He saw no one else, Signorina."

Tally moved with precision and purpose. "You said the police in St. Croix would have jurisdiction for this investigation. When do they take over?"

"Perhaps tomorrow." Abruptly, Vincenzo's tone changed, "My hands, how you say, are full?"

He looked at the door. "That was an update. Down below, in the crew quarters, just before we found Signorina Phelps, we found a dead crewman in his cabin. A Haitian boy, on his first cruise."

"Murdered?" Tally asked feeling an involuntary rush of dread.

Vincenzo's look was tired, exhausted. "The doctor has just completed a peripheral examination. There are no outward signs of purposeful death, however, he is merely a general practitioner and has no knowledge, other than the obvious, of wrongful death. The possibility of a contagious disease, I admit, is remote. The young man was given vaccinations and an extensive exam just weeks ago. Should I not resolve both deaths by two o'clock tomorrow afternoon, for the protection of the passengers, the captain has received orders to return to the United States. At this point, the chance of us docking in St. Croix is slim at best."

"This is just great. First, Tally thinks the woman of my dreams may be the Caribbean strangler, and now my whole damned vacation may be in jeopardy." Cid smashed her cigarette in a glass ashtray and started for the door. "I need another drink."

"Hold on." Vincenzo rubbed the bridge of his nose. "I have many things to do. Cidney, I need your help and Signorina Tally's as well. I'm in, how you say, over my head. Facts need to be gathered so final decisions can be made. For now, I have little more than sixteen hours. We must find resolution for these two deaths. Perhaps you could interrogate the friends of the victim. Give me your feelings, your guts."

"Gut instincts," Tally corrected with half a smile. "Under whose authority would we be working?"

"Shipmaster Cruises. I will e-mail my supervisor at once for written approval. I can assure you, you will be generously compensated for your time and the disruption of your vacation."

With an air of hope, he continued. "The friends," he said pointing at Karen Phelps' body, "they would perhaps be more comfortable if another woman, like yourself, were asking the questions?"

"Not in this lifetime," Cid considered him, her blue eyes pools of stubborn thought. She never expected this late in her life, never hoped to find someone to share her retirement years. What she had wanted and needed had leaked away long ago, absorbed by an overbearing mother and countless, faceless victims of murder.

"Too damned much at stake. Not just my vacation," she continued slowly, "but a chance at some fun, maybe a little happiness. Hell, I don't care if I just met Mimi. At my age chances are just that, they don't come often and I'm not wasting my opportunity. I'll cover your butt, Tal, when you need me, but otherwise count me out. Sorry Vinny."

As she eyed Cid, her look of caution said much more than Tally could express.

Vincenzo smoothed his mustache, and cleared his throat openly disappointed in Cid's response. "The death is hours old. I fear, how you say, the trail is getting colder?"

"And the solution probability is going down." Tally added.

He looked at Cid. "I am asking for a favor-one old friend to another."

A tic at the corner of his mouth spoke for the pressure and stress he was feeling. "I will remain in charge, Signorina," he continued with persistence, glancing at Tally. "You will have access to anyone on board ship and free reign to come and go as you please. I'll have the body removed after the passengers have retired for the night and the cabin will be off limits to all personnel except those of us involved in the investigation. I will issue you a security card and codes."

Speaking rapidly, Vincenzo Pallino leaned forward. "My ego is small, Cidney. I have not your talent or experience. I will give you my gratitude and cooperation." Now his head bowed with embarrassment. His face long. "If I don't resolve these deaths, my balls, how you say, will be on the chopping block."

His voice trailed away. Cid looked at him steadily, but said nothing.

Touching the loop of her gold earring, Tally straightened her back and paused. The gesture seemed designed to cover the awkward moment. She felt sorry for him and it showed on her face. "If you want my expertise, Vincenzo, then you'll have to respect the fact that I work independently of your authority. The bottom line here is finding out who murdered Karen Phelps."

She didn't wait for a reply. "I'll give you till two tomorrow afternoon. No more, no less. And you damn well better believe I expect to be well compensated."

Promptly, Tally turned to Cid. "Your camera. I need to borrow it."

"What the hell for?" With considerable effort, Cid stuffed her shirttail in her pants. "Last pictures you took were all sky and feet." She raised her arms and went through an elaborate mime of trying to focus the camera.

They all laughed, breaking the tension.

"Vincenzo needs a pathologist, I intend to give him one," Tally finally answered.

"With my Mavica camera?"

"Vincenzo's online and if his computer is truly 'top of the line', then he has digital capabilities. I'll scan the pictures in and send them to Harry," Tally explained, referring to San Francisco chief medical examiner Harry Sinclaire. "He can download the material on his computer."

Pushing her hand through her strawberry bangs, Tally calculated. "The whole process shouldn't take more than thirty minutes."

"Magnifico!" Vincenzo declared.

Turning, she looked at Cid. "We have to start somewhere and since you're critical of my camera technique," Tally tried to sound aggrieved, "you could stay...take pics of Phelps' body."

Cid looked at her with a combination of irritation and cool amusement. She was a private citizen now; it wasn't her responsibility to play cop. Yet, this was home, what she knew best. She had a cop's blood and couldn't resist the chase. She felt the familiar rush. The excitement. The challenge. In her gut the chase was on and she was one of the hunters. She took a last look around the room. "Shit."

5

Saturday, July 11
9:27 p.m.

She searched the hall, her head pressed against the wall, the door open no more than an inch. Someone passed in the corridor; a woman laughed. Next door, a toilet flushed.

Calculating the possibility that the occupants of the suite would return before she was through, she had picked up a small dish of mints in another cabin and placed them on the table. It was the perfect cover if needed.

Later, after an indeterminate amount of time, the door to suite seventeen opened. She watched Cid leave first, then a few minutes later the short man, hunched and bald, and finally Tally.

She was uneasy. It wasn't going the way she had planned. She had not counted on the interference of the two private detectives. More worrisome was Tally. She appeared to be the ringleader.

After her brief initial shock, she decided she had little to fear. She felt alert, sharp and determined. She would eliminate Tally and, if her chubby friend, Cid, persisted in her investigation afterwards, she would kill her too. Her resolve became steely. Like the others, she would plan the murder coldly and logically. There would be no mistakes. No guilt.

The vivid memories, the pain of years ago were pushed aside. She was beginning to feel the power, an almost drunken exaltation.

6

Saturday, July 11
9:41 p.m.

Hidden in the bowels of the ship, next to the engine room, Vincenzo Pallino's small office was dark-paneled and lined with bookshelves containing hundreds of paperback volumes. Idle hours at sea passed in the printed world of mystery, science fiction and, Tally noted with surprise, even a little romance.

Another wall held a computer station complete with printer, fax, telephone and an array of international police periodicals. The décor was not sophisticated. There was no sign of family pictures. No personnel effects. A pair of handcuffs dangled from a small pegboard next to the desk. In the far corner of the room, a locked gun cabinet held three 9mm Glocks, a single Luger, a tray of clips, and a half a dozen Bulgarian AK-47s. The automatic rifles were an illegal weapon in the United States, but not for a ship of Panamanian registry like the Sea Pearl.

To the average traveler, the arsenal would have seemed ridiculously out of place. However, hanging on the wall, a framed picture of the *Achille Lauro* served as a grim reminder that the threat of terrorism was a constant reality.

Tally pushed the frightening thoughts from her mind and let her attention drift. In some ways, the room reminded her of their own cozy library in the bayside condominium she and Katie shared. It was their favorite room, high ceilings, with cedar bookcase walls and a large fireplace made of natural rock gathered from the seashore in Half Moon

Bay. It was a safe, warm place seldom invaded by anything more harmful than the details contained within the volumes.

Tally smiled at the thought as she parked a hip on the corner of the desk and reached for the telephone, punched in her cabin number and waited for Katie to answer.

Even now, after all of their months together, Tally realized that there was a part of her that found Katie's affection, their intimacy, a gift. She loved their nakedness together; loved Katie's touch, the feel of her heartbeat against her breasts. There was a warm permanence about Katie that Tally cherished. As if by reflex, Tally shut her eyes. She was still for a time, happy with the visual effects her mind conjured up.

Silent and disappointed, Tally hung up after six rings. She was glad Katie was out enjoying herself, but just hearing her voice would have made the tasks that lay ahead so much easier.

She took a seat in a comfortable brown leather chair, swiveled and leaned back, long slender legs up on the corner of the desk, and placed her ship-to-shore call.

Idly, Tally traced the edge of the handcuffs with her finger while a receptionist at the San Francisco Hall of Justice paged the chief medical examiner in the autopsy theater.

"Sinclaire here." Harry's voice was tinged with his own degree of exhaustion. Short and stout and amiably gliding into his sixties, Harry was a workachohlic with a reputation for excellence in a career that dealt with violence, the macabre and the unlucky. After witnessing years of brutal misery, he still believed most of humankind to be good. Only at home, in the quiet, when his mind was unguarded, did the ghosts come back to haunt.

A long-standing family friend, Harry had become a confidant and surrogate father to Tally shortly after her own father's violent death. It was a role he not only enjoyed, but relished.

"Hey," he said with renewed energy after hearing Tally's bubbly hello, "got the pictures. Can't give you a lot of details, I could only spare about ten minutes. Computer shots were clear and the camera work was topnotch. Close-up of the eyes and neck area was brilliant. Tell Cid I was impressed."

"Right now she's taking shots of the second body I told you about, the Haitian boy. I'll send the pictures as soon as she's through. Believe me when I say, she is less than happy that her vacation has been interrupted."

There was a second's pause and then the echo of delayed transmission. "Well I can't say as I blame her," he offered flatly.

Tally wasn't sure, but she thought she heard a faint rebuke beneath Harry's words.

He cleared his throat. "There was an explosion down at the wharf earlier today. Fishing boat took out half of Pier 19. Six casualties. Looks like drugs might be involved. Police commissioner is all over me. I need to get back to work." His voice took on the tone of a seasoned professional.

Tally pulled her notepad from her pocket and began taking notes. Harry started relaying details almost immediately.

"There are several areas of petechial hemorrhages. Neck, face, eyes. Death appears to be from strangulation with partial decapitation as a result." An air of grimness trailed his words.

"If you look closely on the right side of the throat you will see a quarter of an inch of small black or dark wire protruding. Not copper in nature. Take a look at it, Tal, could be the picture, but it looks odd. Could be cabling. Definitely the murder weapon. Probably broke under the force applied by the assailant. Death would have been slow for the victim. Three, maybe five minutes.

"There is also a tiny cut on the right side of the neck, just below the initial deep tissue wound. It's really more of an indentation, the type of injury we see when intense pressure is being applied, as it was in this case. The pattern is consistent with the assailant having worn a ring. If the victim were here, I'd excise the area and get it under a scope. Sometimes we get lucky." Harry was decisive, his memory flawless.

"A number of years ago I had a case where a housewife had been strangled with her bathrobe belt. The force of the attack had been so intense it not only snapped the victim's neck, it left the impression of her husband's class ring embedded in her flesh. He's a lifer now."

Her voice rising sharply, Tally said, "I don't have a scope, Harry, and as Cid is fond of saying, 'The dead ain't talking.' Tell me more about the ring."

"I'm looking at computer pictures and laser prints, everything is supposition," he answered tersely. "The injury is compact which would suggest the ring or, more precisely, the stone is small in nature. Beyond that, your guess is as good as mine."

"Could a woman have committed this murder?" Tally asked in a low voice.

"The depth of the wound would suggest masculine power. Still, it might have been an extremely strong woman."

The eerie quiet and the subtle swaying of the boat left Tally feeling uneasy. "Is there more?"

"No evidence of defense injuries, no cuts or bruises. Minor abrasions on both feet. The star on the buttocks was carved postmortem. The dermis is white, meaning the heart had already stopped pumping. No teeth marks. And this was no carve-em-up job. Pure articulate surgery, as good as any plastic surgeon.

"It appears the victim was about five-foot two. The angle of the wire is upward. I'd say the perpetrator was moderately tall, no less than five-feet eight." Harry's pause was punctuated with phone static. "Without X-rays, I'm out on a limb. Several of the victim's fingers appear to be at odd angles."

"I don't get it. What are you saying, Phelps had arthritis?"

"No," Harry continued grimly. "At some point the hands were tied and it appears several of the fingers violently broken. Twist fractures. That could suggest a certain sadistic ferocity to this crime."

Tally felt a hollow fear. "But why?"

"That's not my specialty, Sweetheart. Give Grayson Chandler a call. He's the profiler."

Tally kneaded her temples as she gazed out the tiny porthole across the room. The tops of small aqua waves turned white as they nipped at the glass. She could almost see Karen Phelps in life, feel her horrified fear, hear her pleas for reason. "Doesn't the pain ever get to you, Harry? The senselessness of it all?"

His voice was weary. "There's been times. After all of these years if I didn't still feel the horror and the pity, I would have changed jobs long ago. Now I focus on retirement." Harry laughed, his mind instinctively rejecting the dark shadows.

"When we were young, your father and I pledged not to retire until we were ninety and had total control over the city. We saw ourselves as young tycoons in the making-too smart and too ambitious to fail. That was way before we understood the forces behind messy bureaucracy. The frailties of life.

"Hell, who knows, maybe I'll plead stress-related insanity, retire tomorrow, and whisk your mother from her society digs and off on a cruise of our own. You know I took Victoria to the Coit Ball last weekend? We actually had a pleasant evening."

"You and Mother went on a date?" Tally didn't know whether to laugh or applaud.

Harry's long-distance voice sounded faintly jolly. "We struck a bargain. I agreed to wear a tux and she agreed to a hot dog at the Hungry Hound afterwards. Victoria's a nice woman. I feel badly that I never took the time to really know her when your father was alive. In some ways life has cheated her," Harry said with casual certainty. "Patrick was a good man, he was just an overachiever who came home burned out with nothing left for his family. It's no wonder your mother has always flittered from one charitable cause to another. It fills her hours and validates her goodness."

The not-so-tacit remark was without judgment, yet it found its way to Tally's heart. For a moment, with sadness, Tally thought of her mother, alone, in her huge Edwardian house in Pacific Heights-the home where Tally had become who she was now. Somewhere between Tally's childhood and the present, she realized, her mother had grown in dignity, but lost her smile. For years, it had been her father, who, for Tally, defined what love was. Now, with sudden clarity, she realized her mother had been the one always there.

"Thank you for showing Mother a good time. This disrespectful child will give her a call later this evening," Tally said, realizing with foolish surprise that Harry was smitten.

"Glad to hear you're calling. It'll give Victoria a boost. Gotta go, Tal, the dead are waiting."

"Hold on," Tally pleaded with warmth. "One more favor. Can you call Grayson and tell him what you just told me?"

"Tal!"

"Tell him I'll track him down in about twenty minutes."

"Who," Harry asked in a droll tone, "is going to be your patsy when I retire?"

"Certainly not some ruthless tycoon. And certainly not someone I love as much as you."

Like so many things in Tally's life, her friendship with Grayson Chandler led back to her father. In a special way, Dr. Chandler was also part of the McGinnis clan. He had shared a small house in Palo Alto with Patrick McGinnis while both were still in school at Stanford. Patrick studied law, Grayson medicine with a duel specialty in psychiatry/criminology.

For Patrick, after graduation offers poured in from prestigious law firms, but he preferred public service with an eye toward political office. He fully intended to take his society bride and daughter Tally to the California governor's mansion one day and perhaps even the White House. He believed if he did the right thing for his constituents, all would come out for the best in the end. He was naively mistaken and it cost him his life when a barrage of bullets shattered the silence of his office one golden San Francisco day.

Grayson Chandler, on the other hand, had been heavily recruited by the FBI National Academy in Quantico, Virginia. Suspect profiling was a new field at the time and he quickly became an international star.

After ten years he returned to San Francisco because it best served his ambitions. He was an exceptionally skilled psychiatrist and grew wealthy from his private practice. But, for the law enforcement community, one fact remains paramount: He is a superb suspect profiler and his skills, even today, are in constant demand.

If Patrick had been Tally's role model, then Grayson was surely her center of gravity, and, after twenty years of friendship, Tally's motives were as familiar to Grayson Chandler as the young lawyer he had roomed with in college. He knew her instincts for investigation and crime resolution were nearly as powerful as her desire to touch people and make their lives better. He also was keenly aware of Tally's stubborn streak, her tenacious need to try and correct the world's wrongs, to solve every crime, every murder. Although he found her ambitions admirable, he also was concerned that she seldom took time for herself or those she loved.

"Murder on the high seas," Grayson began, his voice a soothing chant. "Sounds like a plot from an Agatha Christie novel. And, if you'll excuse the pun, in my opinion, attempting to solve a murder while on a luxury liner is going a bit overboard."

Tally rolled her eyes toward the ceiling. A small chuckle escaped her lips. She could imagine Grayson leaning back in his overstuffed office chair, stroking his white goatee, the waist of his linen suit straining from his wide girth.

"Well, you have to admit, at least I have a captive group of suspects," she countered.

This time the doctor laughed. "This is true, as long as your killer isn't into marathon swimming."

Abruptly, Grayson seemed bored with banter. "I have the crime scene pictures on my computer and I'm making prints as we speak. The victim profile is limited to age, occupation, home town and physical characteristics."

Grayson was quiet for a moment. His breathing was labored from asthma that was always worse during the summer months.

"The crime scene is relatively bland, which may be part of the offender's strategy or traits. Yet, even the most mundane clues offer a potential window into the murder's soul. They always leave their emotions at the scene. No matter how good or careful the offender may be, they can't help but leave part of their personality behind. I suspect the noose is closely related to the killer's relationship with the victim. The murderer has probably fantasized this crime for years, perhaps at some point even threatened the victim." He enunciated slowly. "The room heat could be as simple as the killer's need to control the environment-all the ducks in a row."

There was a significant amount of static on the line. "Comparatively, the emotions surrounding the perpetrator are blatant. The victim was tightly bound and strangulation ferocious. An offender, who not only needed to control, but also took pleasure in watching the suffering, as evidenced by the wrist bruising and the deep neck wounds. The star is simple egotism. A job well done. I suspect the bondage was released postmortem. The broken fingers would suggest torture. A payback perhaps. You hurt me, now I'm going to hurt you."

"An old lover?" Tally asked solemnly.

"Certainly a possibility." Grayson paused again. "Or a friend or co-worker. There are no defense injuries, which would suggest at some point the victim felt a certain misconceived comfort zone. She knew her attacker well enough not to fear."

"What about the fact she was nude? Wouldn't that also suggest she shared an intimate relationship with the killer?" Tally asked.

"Not necessarily. I don't see this as a crime of passion. The killer could have undressed the victim after she was dead. Leaving her nude may have been the final insult: a literal stripping away of dignity."

Her jaw firmly set, Tally was staring off. For a moment she allowed sorrow to own her.

"The damage to the body is minimal. I don't sense rage here," the doctor continued, "which may imply a female killer. Women tend to be much less violent than men when externalizing their anger. I also sense a peculiar respect. This is not a stranger murder. The body was left posed on the floor. The room is neat, as if there were an understanding: a regard for likes and dislikes.

"This predator, in all probability, is very intelligent. She's not a serial killer, rather someone who is trying to get her message across. Someone with an axe to grind. These killings are about power not just a sudden window of opportunity opening. There were no mistakes or tip-offs with this crime, which suggests meticulous organization. A certain logic is also clearly evident, which makes me believe the killer is not youthful. The lack of evidence suggests the perpetrator is someone with a previous criminal history. She's not new at this. MO is learned behavior."

When Tally didn't reply he continued.

"I am perplexed by the bookmark left on the victim's thigh. Obviously the murderer intended it as a message. A clue or perhaps even a warning. This behavior would be consistent with a classic Adlarian, a killer determined to control all the elements."

He let that sink in for a moment.

"Harry also mentioned a note sighting the 'Three Blind Mice' rhyme." Grayson went on. "This could mean the killer sees herself as a leader, a savior if you will. Jim Jones of the Peoples' Temple comes to mind. Ultimate power over his flock. When Jones' supremacy was threatened, he successfully advocated mass suicide. At some point in time, your shipboard killer was awakened to the fact that her power over her flock was not as influential as she believed. She could have been abandoned or perhaps ridiculed for her attempts at supremacy and power. "Hearts of ice" would suggest she has been terribly hurt and thinks people did not forgive her. Her pain and anger has festered over time and now she has come back to avenge whatever perceived misdeeds were perpetrated against her. If more than one person has left a fingerprint on the offender's mind, I have no doubt, there will be multiple victims."

7

Saturday, July 11
10:02 p.m.

Cid stopped, eyes wide open in distress. "Jesus, Vinny, it's colder than a dead mackerel in here." She could see her breath as she spoke and the cool rawness was a shock. She slapped at the goose flesh on her arms as she glanced around the dull-gray walk-in-cooler.

The small enclosure held two long shelves just wide enough to accommodate a good-sized body. Juvention Herrero lay to the right covered by a white sheet. One arm was cocked at an odd angle, rigor mortis holding it stiffly in place. A thermometer, a pair of scissors and a black body bag lay on the other shelf.

They were silent for a time. Even for career cops used to mindless brutality, there are always those first moments of hollow comprehension when conversation does not come easy.

The distinctive odor of Pine-sol was overpowering. Although the refrigeration unit was seldom used for its intended purpose, no amount of cleaning disinfectants or deodorizer could camouflage the noxious odor of death. Vincenzo held his gloved hands to his nose grateful for the heavy latex smell.

Cid noticed a small amount of spittle and vomit covered the side of Juvention's face, as she slowly pulled the white sheet from the body. The stench was strong, but she had smelled corpses that were worse.

She looked blankly at Vincenzo. "I thought you said the doctor'd already checked out the stiff. Done an exam. Hell, doesn't look like the clothes have been touched."

"Scusa," Vincenzo said with a confused laugh. "Peripheral exam only. Shipmaster Cruises must be careful. If we overstep our authority we could, how you say, face litigation from the family. Capisce?" He regretted his frankness immediately and it showed.

Cid felt a rush of irritation. "Don't jack me around, Vinny." She pointed her gloved finger at the chief of security. "Let me see if I've got this straight. You expect Tally and I to put our vacations and God knows what the hell else on the line, while you and Shipmaster Cruises sit back and protect your little asses? Bullshit! That's not only self-serving, it's an insult to your integrity."

She spoke smoothly now, a smirk on her lips that could not be mistaken for a smile. "You're a grown man. How you deal with the political pressures of your job is your choice. But don't expect any help from me if you're not going to play fair and square."

She looked at him blandly, fired up a cigarette and let smoke slowly drift from her nose. She knew from experience that the first hours or days of an investigation were hardest. People lied. Players jockeyed for positions of importance. Investigators looked for direction and purpose. Methods and procedures were often dumped because of intrusion from head honchos who set unrealistic guidelines and demands. For someone as rigidly disciplined as Cid, politics were unbearable. Yet, she knew the drill well, had turned in her badge because of the politicos, and now felt a certain empathy for her friend Vinny.

His lips parted, but no sound emerged. Respectfully he met her intense glare and nodded a silent apology. Cid saw the shame, embarrassment on his face before it slipped behind a wall of professionalism.

Even with the cooler hovering around thirty-eight degrees, tiny beads of perspiration formed just under Vincenzo Pallino's eyes as he reached for the scissors and began cutting away Juvention Herrero's busboy uniform.

"Politics exist in every organization." Cid's voice was flat, yet forgiving, as she rested her hand on Vincenzo's shoulder. She knew the stress of political pressure from inside and outside any police organization and she knew any minor misstep could mean the end of a career.

"I'm not insensitive to the difficult position you're in and, if I were you, Vinny, I'd resent the hell out of my big mouth."

Pleasant man that he was, Vincenzo did not look offended as he continued his task. Being in charge of security on board a ship required cooperation between various police agencies. Vincenzo had learned early on when to protect his territory and when to back off.

"I admire your candor, to say nothing of your keen investigative mind." He looked up, his eyes twinkling. "As far as your mouth..." He let out an exaggerated groan and let the matter drop.

His gloved fingers grazed cold skin as the arms and neck were exposed first. A small, gold charm attached to a thin leather cord fell into view. Cid quietly studied the trinket before slipping it over the victim's head and into her pocket for closer viewing at a later time. At the belt line, Vincenzo began slicing through a cotton, white shirt.

Cid watched silently. Juvention Herrero was tall with a stocky build, she noted and she guessed, somewhere between twenty-five and thirty. His hands were hard and worn. His hair more brown than black and his skin pale and freckled. Although there was a quality to his appearance that suggested his black Haitian nativeness, she was sure he was of mixed race. But what struck her at the moment, was the smoothness of his face and his delicate features. He was pretty.

As Vincenzo clipped from hem to collar, the shirt fell open and to the side. An audible gasp escaped his mouth. He backed off looking closely at Cid, trying to read information she was still trying to process.

Juvention Herrero's chest was bound with several ace bandages and a fair amount of old-fashioned, white adhesive tape.

Cid tossed her cigarette in a gray bucket in the corner of the cooler and calmly took the scissors from Vincenzo. She easily cut through the ace bandages and flicked them to the side. Small lovely breasts with rich, brown nipples popped into view. Cid was merely surprised by their discovery; Vincenzo was bewildered.

"Someone is gonna catch alota flak on this one."

Together they undressed her. There were no obvious wounds, but there was a distinct odor. Cid leaned closer.

"What is it?" he asked.

She shook her head, alarm clearly evident in her expression. "I'm not sure. Something strong." She walked to the cooler door and pushed it open. "Could be a junkie with a snootful of shit. Could be something toxic. Whatever, I wouldn't hang in this cooler for long."

"Si." Vincenzo Pallino answered, barely able to contain his urge to bolt.

"I thought you said crew members had complete medical exams just weeks ago." Cid asked evenly, unable to remove her eyes from the corpse. "Seems to me even a quack could tell the difference between a man and a woman."

"Examines and inoculations are given prior to employment, but not," he quickly added, "by Shipmaster Cruises. A valid examination form and full documentation of vaccinations must be submitted to the cruise line by a licensed medical doctor. Perhaps money exchanged hands in Port-au-Prince."

Cid shrugged. "Does Shipmaster check passports and paperwork when new crew board ship?"

"Si. Everything is meticulous."

"Really?" Cid's eyes were troubled. "Well, someone sure as hell fucked up this time." She looked closely at a small butterfly tattoo on the dead woman's left breast and noted the initials SS. "Any friends, acquaintances on board?"

"Not that we have found. He, scusa, she boarded ship this morning with an older woman she introduced as her mother. She picked up her assignment and keys and once she entered her cabin, the stewards did not see her again."

"And the mother?"

"Would have disembarked prior to sailing."

"The mother lived in Miami?" Cid asked easily, the wheels turning, "and you've notified her of the death?"

Vincenzo hesitated. "The crew was told, at the time the temporary guest pass was issued, that the mother was visiting a cousin in Miami. No address was given." The chief of security looked stung now.

"Any identification, personal affects found in the cabin? Any sign of forced entry?"

"No, the door to the cabin was not damaged." Vincenzo's eyes were wary. "And we found nothing. No personal items. Not a comb or brush or even the extra uniforms and master keys provided by the cruise line. Any paperwork--family address, references and passport--filed with Shipmaster has thus far proved to be, how you say, bogus."

"No clothes or keys" Cid repeated thoughtfully. "How do you figure that?"

"A thief perhaps." His voice trailed away.

"Nah." Cid pointed at the body. "Someone's gone to far, too much trouble for this kill to be a simple robbery. Besides you said no forced entry. Roll her prints, Vinny, we may get lucky, she might have a prior."

"Do you think we will catch him...the killer?" he asked.

"Him? You think the murderer is a man?"

"Si. Women, how you say, are soft, gentle souls. They break your heart, but seldom kill."

Cid frowned with a tired familiarity. Violence against woman was a wound that never healed. There were too many women battered, killed, and forgotten. Still, the comment, the implied inferiority, even surrounding such a grisly issue, lingered in the gloomy enclosure. Her annoyance showed before she could check it. "Women are smarter than men. Plan better...don't get caught as often. But don't fool yourself, Vinny, we're not only capable of running corporations and countries...berserko's come in all forms and have a rational all their own."

8

Saturday, July 11
10:25 p.m.

Outside, moonlight spread white on the water as Tally took long purposeful strides through the brightly-lit colonnade that led to the casino and several lounges.

Pulsating hip hop rolled out the door of one cabaret, soft jazz from a small piano bar, and the cheerful beat of calypso echoed down the wide corridor from the Island Lounge. Woman snickered and held hands, some sang along with favorite tunes. Lovers cuddled together, enjoying the simple delight of touching each other.

Tally watched women go by, old couples laughing and talking, young couples lounging at small tables. She now understood why Katie had been so sure, so adamant they take a lesbian cruise. There was a simple shared joy; an interwoven pride of being lesbian displayed in sensual touching, smiles and laughter. A wonderful sisterhood that made her feel proud.

Still, Tally could not shake the dull, well-worn reel of movie film that played over and over in her head. Karen Phelps was the star and the images tormented her. She thought of Karen's wasted education and her family who surely would be shattered when they heard of their loss. Of friends who would mourn and miss her. She wondered if there was a lover who would now be alone. It was the little things that brought it home for Tally, and made murder personal.

They agreed earlier to meet outside the ship's liquor store. Cid arrived first, Tally a few seconds later. The liquor store or Duty Free Shop sat nestled between a tobacco store and a jewelry showroom, whose specialty, Tally read, was emeralds.

Even with the hour late, an older Hispanic woman sat at a small table just inside the tobacco shop, hand, rolling cigars. Tally and Cid watched for a few minutes, fascinated by the agility of the woman's wrinkled and knotted fingers. A sign over her table declared: "La Gloria Cubana-hand rolled cigars from the United States and the Dominican Republic."

Languidly the woman smiled, displaying a short freshly rolled cigar between stained fingers. "Robusto," she said, as if savoring the feel. "Smooth, light and flavorful. Only seven dollars. You try?"

Tally laughed at that, looking into the cigar-makers vivid brown eyes, flirting a little. She had never dreamed of smoking a cigar and found the idea less than pleasurable. "Maybe next time," she offered with a smile.

Lighting a cigarette, Cid eyed the cigar through the flame of a long wooden match she plucked from a basket next to a row of freshly rolled cigars. "Why not?" she said boldly, holding up two fingers. She dropped the match into a large ashtray, slid a twenty across the table and waved off the change, stuffing the cigars proudly in her breast pocket.

"Make sure I'm about six blocks away when you light those up," Tally said backing out the door.

Cid shook her head in mock dismay, waving to the cigar-maker as they left. "You don't know what you're missn', girl, pure pleasure."

For a moment they were comfortably silent, the routine of two old friends taking time to gather their thoughts. Then they carefully debriefed each other.

After a while Cid reached in her pocket and pulled out the small gold charm she had taken from the dead Haitian woman. "Ever see anything like this before?"

Tally's face was attentive now. She took several seconds to carefully inspect the object. Two serpents with sparkling diamond-chip eyes, wrapped around a gold winged staff. There were several smooth spots on the charm, suggesting both age and wear. "A caduceus." She said at length.

Cid glanced at her. "A what?" Her posture and expression were that of a master mentor raptly listening to her illustrious student.

"A caduceus. It's the symbol for the medical profession. Doctors, nurses, even dentists wear them on their white coats or uniforms. I've never seen one with diamonds." Tally paused, shaking her head in wonderment, "The Haitian woman was wearing this?"

"Yes."

"And she's not a doctor?"

For what seemed a long while, Cid searched her memory. "Nah," she finally answered. "The Haitian's hands were rough and callused, more like a laborer. Didn't have a polished look." She folded her arms across her chest, feeling the cigars in her pocket.

"Do you think the two deaths are connected?" Tally asked, her voice falling to half a whisper.

"Anything's possible, 'specially considering this little doctor trinket." Cid paused, blue eyes narrowing, as if sorting something out. "But I don't get the disguise and how a young Haitian woman would connect with a doctor from Milwaukee."

Pausing, Cid shook her head, the dead woman's image etched in her memory. "She was a big woman. Could have fought off any attacker, but hell, there was no violence. No cuts, no bruises. The only odd thing was the smell," Cid continued abstractly, leaning against a white wall awash in hot pink neon. "Garlic. Smelled like a pot of your spaghetti sauce. Could be arsenic." Her cigarette wagged in her mouth as if she were conducting a symphony.

"But you're thinking some kind of poison rather than a disease?" Tally asked suddenly restless, aware women were more apt to use poison or knifes when they killed.

Cid shrugged playing with the idea. "Maybe she was a bimbo with a nose full of smack. But she didn't have that gray druggie look. I checked her arms and legs. Clean. She looked cared for and healthy. Even had a little butterfly tattoo on her breast; letters SS were on the

wing. Could be her initials." Cid seemed distracted by her own thoughts. .
"And why the hell the missing uniforms?"

They stood in silence for a moment, the tiny decorative lights
from the duty free shop blinking and winking at them.

As Tally moved closer, Cid's eyes followed her. "Let's assume,
for now, the deaths are related. Same killer." She suggested.

Cid scratched her head. "So you're saying the perp took the
uniforms? Not exactly the pawnshop top-five."

"No." Tally paused, considering. "You said a set of master
keys was missing also?"

Cid nodded.

"What if the keys and uniforms were taken randomly?" Tally's
voice held patience. The cadence of one logical word falling into place
after another. "We have absolutely no clue as to the Haitian victim's
identity. A Jane Doe. Maybe that's what the killer intended. When the
room was swept clean of personal affects, could be, the uniforms and
keys became part of the cover-up."

Frowning, Cid flicked her ashes in a large shell- shaped
cement ashtray. "I can't get a handle on this, Tal. Two women chilled
and no logical connector. Far as I can tell, nothing of value was stolen,
so greed wasn't an issue. It stands to reason Phelps and the Haitian
woman weren't lovers, so jealousy is a low probability for motive. Same
goes for rejection or revenge. So why the kills?"

Tally gazed up at the ceiling, as if to reconstruct her thought
process. Homicides were generally the results of great passions or very
sick minds determined to make a statement in blood. But these
murderers were different. Neat, quick, very little violence. And the
status issue bothered Tally too. A prosperous doctor and a member of
the crew. A woman dressed as a man. Why?

"Drug-running is a possibility," Tally cocked her head, "but the
evidence doesn't seem to add up. Still, drugs mean big money and
when you live in a poor country, like Haiti, masquerading as a busboy
would be a piece of cake when you consider the payoff."

Tally mulled this over. "But it seems to me, if someone wanted
to smuggle drugs past customs, the Haitian woman would have been
more valuable alive than dead, which brings us back to square one."

Cid looked up. "Which is?"

"The note left in Phelps' suite. The note I believe Mimi wrote." Tally had no axe to grind, just a gut sense that something lay beneath the surface of the letter and right now she was willing to grasp at any straw that would lead her to the killer.

Cid gave a shrug of irritation, her face hard. "Fact is, anybody with the initials 'M' could have written the note."

Tally smiled ruefully.

There comes a point in a murder investigation when there are more muddled clues than the mind can assimilate. Some homicide detectives write everything down: neat little dossiers of each victim. It doesn't bring crime solution closer, but it does lend itself to order. Tally jotted a few things that bothered her in her notebook and then walked over to the windowed wall that ran the length of the corridor. Cupping her hands around her eyes she looked out. The water was inky black, the moon framed by a half-circle of gray clouds. Something was nagging at her mind, something she had heard or seen. A clue felt, but not recognized.

"Suppose," Tally spoke with cool precision as she turned to face Cid, "the Haitian woman was a pawn?"

Cid stood straighter. "How so?"

Tally stopped a moment and reflected. "You said someone else boarded ship with the Haitian woman. Someone who claimed to be her mother. Maybe she wasn't her mother. Maybe the Haitian woman was her ticket to get on board. And just maybe she never got off the ship and is hiding somewhere…maybe in a certain dinner companion's room."

She was quiet for a moment. Cid, Tally saw, was listening intently. "Maybe the stowaway is using the stolen uniforms as cover and used the master keys to get into Karen Phelps' room to kill her."

"Jesus, Tal, you've been taking to much Dramamine." Cid stiffened, moving back a couple of steps. Both her tone and posture bespoke astonishment. "You really believe Mimi would hide a killer in her room? Get real."

"I never mentioned Mimi this time."

"Bullshit! You inferred as much." Her hands clenched and her eyes rested on Tally until her face was stiff with anger.

Tally felt a surge of shame. "I'm sorry," she said softly, "I should have been more specific. We need to set up a meet with all the college roommates."

Cid raised her head; her profile was agitated. "I've got a date, remember?" She took a long, impatient drag on her cigarette and thrust the butt in the ashtray with such force a few grains of sand popped on the floor. "And these damn things taste like alligator shit."

Tally was no stranger to Cid's anger, only this time it had a fair amount of hurt attached to it. Watch it, Tally wanted to say. Watch your heart, but instead Tally was moved by the emotions she read in Cid's eyes. She touched her shoulder. "One quick stop at the duty free shop and I'll help you find Mimi."

The Duty Free Store displayed a panoramic view of bottled spirits, crystal decanters and lovely hand-cut crystal glasses. A few potted palms lined the windows and accented display cases.

While Cid perused the large selection of Scotch, Tally waited for a customer to finish with a purchase and then stepped up to the cash register and identified herself.

"How may I help Madam?" asked an attractive man with a lyrical British accent.

"A gift basket with an expensive bottle of 1970 Chateau Lafite Rothschild was delivered to suite seventeen shortly after we sailed. Who made the purchase and was there a gift card enclosed?"

He looked up, stared directly into her face and said politely, "I am sure Madam would not mind if I check with security before supplying such information." His voice held relentless patience.

Tally nodded.

Only when he put down the phone did the cashier look at her again. He thumbed through a number of white charge slips and returned to the counter holding one. "You were correct, Madam, the wine was of very fine quality. The cost of the gift basket was $525.00 American dollars and was purchased by a Ms. Brooks, on the Starfish Deck, cabin 421. The attached card read: 'It's time to forgive.'"

9

Saturday, July 11
11:12 p.m.

She takes pleasure in her anonymity, fading into the crowd, eyes alert and a little amused, always watching and waiting for the right moment.

A pleasant breeze from a gathering storm brought the smell of the sea indoors. At one time she would have found this sort of evening enchanting. Now it was merely a distraction to the hunt. Her body was now in command of all her actions. Her thoughts blunted by hatred and revenge.

She watched Tally, her red-blond hair swaying with the rhythm of her long strides, her athletic good looks stirring the attention of other women.

She noticed Tally slip her arm around her friend Cid. There was kindness in Tally's eyes as she gave the rumpled one a friendly hug. At another time, in another place, she would have found this simple act of kindness endearing. Now, she realized with a jolt, it enraged her. Friendship is nothing more than a means for betrayal!

She feels the coil of cabled wire in her pocket and knows what she must do. She will find a dark place, maybe an empty cabin. She imagines Tally's voice and, like the others, hears her beg for her life. She knows she isn't psychotic. Knows exactly what she must do. She has become what she used to fear, a predator stalking.

10

Saturday, July 11
11:12 p.m.

A saucer of blue smoke floated over the dance floor as the din of Garth Brook's "Friend's in Low Places" spilled out of the Alamo Tavern. The motif inside was western, with branding irons, rope lassos and guitars hung on the wall for decoration. Amber glass lanterns cast a mellow romantic haze across the small room and onto the tiny dance floor.

On their quest to find Mimi, Cid had been restless. The gloomy possibility that she had misread Mimi's intentions grew to unreasonable proportions as she and Tally trekked from one watering hole to another. Finally, on their fourth stop, their search came to a successful conclusion. Cid's disposition changed from the Grim Reaper, to a high school kid on her first date.

Declining an invitation to join her, Tally now watched Cid cut a path to a table in the back corner of the bar. The room was crowded, charged with music and conversation. Young love. Old love. Women relaxing and enjoying themselves. She could see only a few faces, but there was no mistaking Mimi Wingate's smile when she stood to greet Cid--two would-be lovers searching each other out.

With drinks plentiful and the atmosphere affectionate, some intuitive part of Tally wondered how much of what had transpired in Karen Phelps' suite would be extracted from Cid by evening's end.

Her eyes were steady, as Tally looked at Mimi Wingate's cosmetically enhanced face. She saw the smile, the enjoyment, the pleasure she took in making Cid laugh.

Several emotions hit Tally at once: the weight of her own guilt for distrusting Mimi Wingate, agony for Karen Phelps, and enchantment at watching Cid stammer, blush and then laugh uproariously.

Cid pulled the cigars from her breast pocket and ceremoniously presented one to Mimi. Roses, candy or even perfume would have been a more appropriate offering, Tally knew, but the cigars were vintage Cid, her notion of precious bounty.

Smiling, Tally turned away, reflecting wryly on her own loneliness. For an unexplainable instant she felt a chill run through her, the feeling that someone was watching her. She looked around, shrugged and walked over to the long old-fashioned wood bar and picked up the courtesy phone, stabbing in her cabin number and waited. Still no answer. She checked her watch. Replacing the phone in the cradle, concern for Katie nipped at the edge of her mind.

"Howdy. I'd have never pegged you as a country music fan." Cimarron's tone was slightly slurred. She tipped her bottle of Budweiser in Tally's direction. Still wearing her Levi's and yellow cowboy shirt, she fit in perfectly with the western ambience.

"Drowning my sorrow." Cimarron continued, "Nothin' quite like a sad song to make a person feel downright rotten."

"The saga of country music." Tally mustered a smile, but her eyes were sad. "I never got the chance to tell you how sorry I am about the loss of your friend."

Cimarron hesitated, drew a breath. The response seemed heavy, as if Cimarron wanted as much distance from Karen's death as possible.

"Hadn't seen Karen in years. Fact is, I hadn't seen any of the roommates. We all profess to love one another, call ourselves family, but I can't say for sure we even like each other anymore.

"As for Karen, we did the Christmas card routine, but for the most part, the Karen I knew was still an intern at Harborview Hospital in Seattle. The sergeant of our little college household. Her death was a shock and I can't say I'm not sad, but I didn't like Karen when we were college kids and I probably wouldn't have liked her much now."

Tally felt Cimarron's indifference. There was a story in there somewhere and she couldn't help but feel the plot was filled with deep anguish.

Cimarron swallowed the rest of her beer and set the empty bottle on a nearby vacant table. "Can't believe Karen killed herself. She was hell-bent pro-life before the religious right coined the term. Just plain old doesn't make sense." Cimarron was stiff for a moment, as if she said more than she had intended. Using her index finger to swipe her mouth, she then wiped her hand on her pants.

In quick succession, Tally had two impressions: Cimarron's cowboy slang and crudeness was a deliberate misrepresentation of her intelligence, and she seemed guarded, tense. The type of edginess often seen from someone with something to hide.

"What else can you tell me about Karen?" Tally's eyes were steady.

Cimarron hesitated a second and crossed her arms, anger replacing grief. "When I first met you, I found your occupation fascinatin', but to be perfectly honest, down- right unpleasant. The way I see it, people oughta' be able to trod on their own piece of land without havin' to worry about who's gonna snoop in their tracks. Back home my nearest neighbor is some ten miles away. That should tell you I like my privacy. Nosin' around in people's business like you do, diggin' up dirt--maybe even peepin' in windows. That sort of thing doesn't settle well with me. Karen wasn't your friend. What's more, she liked her anonymity."

Cimarron shifted her weight from one foot to the other. "Outside of perhaps some morbid curiosity, I can't figure why Karen's death should be of any interest to you."

The music was louder and the dance floor now crowded. Tally allowed her eyes to stray, letting her silence assert her persistence.

Cimarron turned on Tally caught between anger and despair. "Let Karen rest in peace. She's gone now. She killed herself. No one ever understands that kind of selfishness. Let her take her secrets to the grave. Just back off."

Tally reined in her emotions. She thought Cimarron curiously defensive and was struck by her total lack of sentiment. She leaned her back against the bar and easily slid her hands in the pockets of her khaki pants, subtly letting Cimarron know she wasn't going anywhere and wasn't intimidated by her opinions.

She had learned long ago how to feed tidbits to witnesses and suspects, how to pull them around until they were telling her what she wanted to hear. She made her voice soft and low. "I'm working for ship's security. There's no easy way to say this so we may as well get it out in the open. Karen's death wasn't a suicide. She was murdered. A well-planned killing."

Cimarron became still, alarm butting her face. "I saw her. Saw the noose and that grotesque, bloody ring around her neck." Her face twisted and her eyes flickered with terror as disillusion faded. Shaking she slammed her fist in her palm and clutched her fingers. Her voice rose, "Not another one."

"Another one?"

For a long moment Cimarron was silent.

"At this point," Tally's tone held a quiet intensity, "protecting Karen or anyone else only serves the murderer."

Struggling for self-control, Cimarron nodded. She turned her head slowly and scanned the room. Tally couldn't be certain, but she thought Cimarron looked directly at Mimi Wingate.

Manipulating people without lying was never easy, but Tally was slick. "The sooner you come clean," she pushed, "the better for all concerned. You may know something that could be of great help and not even realize it. Start with the wine. The Chateau Lafite and your note asking forgiveness. Is that one of the secrets you hoped Karen took to her grave?"

For a moment Cimarron watched her, as if deciding whether to stay or go. Her eyes were bleak. "I told you I haven't seen Karen for years."

She stopped talking. The silence was cold.

At length Cimarron began again. "The wine was a peace offerin'." Her voice was filled with vengeance. "I was tryin' to help a friend heal an old wound. As to the secrets Karen took to her grave, I haven't a clue."

She drifted away again and then pulled herself back from some distant, unpleasant place.

"The other death I was referrin' to was Anna's suicide." An uneasy expression crossed her face. "The sorrow of these deaths belong to us. You have no business interferin'. Don't matter much to me who you're workin' for. I don't like what you're doin', and right now I don't like you."

Cimarron's words lacked credibility, but what prickled the hairs on the back of Tally's neck was the way she spoke. Stunned pauses, tremored emotions, undying loyalty. Rehearsed lines. An actress playing to a full house. An actress full of insecurities.

"If a friend of mine were killed, I'd be all over the police or security or whoever was investigating the murder, wanting to know what happened. You haven't asked one question. Why is that? Or do you have all the answers?" Tally asked, her voice clipped.

The music stopped and for a moment the sound of clinking glasses and an occasional roar of laughter was all that could be heard.

Cimarron stared at her. She looked at Tally as if she were something the dog had left behind on the lawn.

"I'm good at what I do, Cimarron." Tally inserted her own dramatic pause. Looked around. "One of the reasons I'm good at my job is because I'm not intimidated by bullies or sucked in by tall tales. Your lack of cooperation is bewildering. $500 is a lot of money to spend for wine for someone you claim not to like. There's also a recent picture of you and Mimi in Karen's suite, which knocks a big hole in your claim not to have recently seen at least some of your college friends. Add all this up and you're becoming a viable suspect in Karen's death."

For a long moment Cimarron was silent-her face a mask.

Tally stared at her, a dozen knife-edge remarks on the tip of her tongue, but she knew better than to push too hard. "There was no sign of a struggle in Karen's suite and no one heard a scream. Logic tells me Karen knew her killer. Make sense?" she asked, her voice now soft, friendly, barely audible.

Cimarron digested this information expressionless.

Still Tally did not raise her voice. She leaned forward slightly, her look warm. "Did Karen have enemies? An old lover maybe?"

Cimarron shrugged.

"Were you Karen's lover?"

The color drained from Cimarron's face.

Tally moved closer. She saw the fear in Cimarron's eyes and it was that which persuaded Tally to go for broke. "And the Haitian woman? How did she connect with Karen?" The question had the impact of a fired gun. Cimarron folded. Fear came into her eyes as the rush of silent memories escaped as if from a dark crevasse. "Ceta?"

Guessing, hoping, Tally nodded.

Cimarron seemed not to breathe and her distress was so raw, Tally stifled the urge to reach out and comfort. Reactively she drew back. Her job was to get information. Break down barriers. Flush out the truth. "Tell me about Ceta," she pushed, all the while intently studying Cimarron.

Cimarron was plainly unsettled, Tally saw. Her shoulders folded in and her crisp yellow shirt suddenly hung limp on her, as if the weight of secrecy were too heavy a burden to carry alone any longer. Beneath the silence, Tally knew, was something much deeper.

"You keep pushin', there's bound to be more bad happen," Cimarron said bitterly.

Warning or apprehension? Tally wondered, letting a little cop grimace appear on her face. She moved toward Cimarron, subtly crowding her space. "Ceta?"

Cimarron felt her bitterness turn to fear. There was a wounded undertone in her voice. "Down a piece, just past the gift shops, there's another bar. The Old Piano Room. I'll get the others and meet you there in thirty minutes." She paused, very still now, as though staring at the crowd without seeing it. She looked down and then seemed to will herself to walk across the bar to where Mimi Wingate sat.

Tally watched. Ignoring Cid, Cimarron bent, whispered in Mimi's ear. Mimi's head snapped upward. Her hands gripped the edge of the table and her eyes darted across the room to where Tally stood. No amount of makeup could hide her concern.

Struggling with conflicting emotions, Tally looked away. She didn't want to dwell on Mimi, wanted her to be innocent of any involvement in the murder of Karen Phelps and the Haitian woman. When she looked back, Cid was puffing on her cigar, her arm draped lazily over Mimi's shoulder.

When Cimarron had gone, Tally waited beside the bar for a short attractive waitress who was finishing a pick-up order. She was carrying a tray of food and two bottles of Heineken when Tally tapped her on the shoulder.

"The table in the back corner with the blond, I'd like to buy them some drinks." Tally dropped a fifty on the tray. "Take twenty for yourself and see that their glasses are kept filled for the next half an hour."

The waitress, her honey-blond hair pulled back in a French braid, flashed a brilliant smile. "Vould you like to pay for this?" She asked with a little more than a trace of a German accent. "It is your friend's order."

Tally glanced at the hamburger and French fries and knew immediately the conglomeration spread with extra mayonnaise and mustard belonged to Cid. The sandwich, she guessed, was Mimi's. "Sure, I'll pay."

The waitress bowed slightly and again flashed her lovely smile. "Cruises are for food und fun. Und soon, your friends vill have the midnight buffet, nein?"

Tally laughed, dropped another twenty on the tray and turned to leave. Suddenly her eyes widened. Jolted, she turned back. "Excuse me," she called.

"Yes," the waitress answered meekly.

"I didn't mean to startle you." Tally pointed at the tray. "The sandwich? What kind is it? Tuna? Roast beef?"

The waitress's eyes puzzled. "Ham."

The image of the plate in Karen Phelps' suite flashed before Tally. "Ham on whole wheat with lettuce and tomato only?"

The waitress bowed her head. "Yes."

Tally's face filled with anguish a sinking sensation in her stomach. "Thank you," she said quietly.

Starring across the room at Mimi, Tally took in a deep breath and shivered.

11

Saturday, July 11
11:50 p.m.

Cid took a long swig of her Heineken, set the bottle on the table and belched loudly. "Good beer," she said without apology.

Mimi tilted her head. "I'll say one thing for you, dearie, you're not pretentious."

"Tally and Katie tell me I'm a little rough around the edges. I guess that comes from living too many years in a shit-hole apartment with only a sweet little dog for a companion." Cid gave a mock wince. "I'm too old to put on airs. What you see is what you get, that includes a few rolls around the middle and decorative cellulite legs."

Picking up her hamburger, Cid tapped her chest. "But the heart is honest and true."

Mimi smiled. Turning, she gazed out at the women dancing. It gave Cid a chance to study her more closely.
There was a tiny mole near her right eye, and her face was fleshy yet had lovely sharp features. She was not conventionally beautiful, but Cid thought her glorious.

When the music stopped, Mimi took a sip of her beer and scrutinized her sandwich before nibbling on the corner.
"Have you ever done anything like this before?"

Cid considered her for a moment. "You mean the cruise or pick up a beautiful woman?"

Suddenly Mimi was laughing again. "The cruise."

"No. But if I'd known what I was missing…" Cid bit into her hamburger wiping the oozing mayonnaise from her mouth with a paper napkin. Her blue eyes twinkled. "Except for your friend Karen, the whole set up, the ship, the food, the women…you. Well hell, it's like a dream come true."

The darkness in Mimi's eyes was softened by the amber lights. "I don't want to talk about Karen."

Around them the smoke and laughter provided a refuge of privacy. Cid took another bite of her hamburger and then pointed with a french fry at Mimi's sandwich. "You're gonna havta' sooner or later. Tally's no fool. I'm sure she saw your sandwich when she paid for our order. Earlier, when I told you Karen was murdered, what I left out was the fact I knew you'd been in Karen's suite." Cid dipped her french fry in a glob of mayonnaise and pushed it in her mouth. "I admire your handwriting. Beautiful. Mine looks like a first-grader scribbling with crayons."

Mimi's eyes filled with fear. She shook her head, silent. Then she rested the side of her face on Cid's shoulder. For Cid, it felt natural, as if Mimi had always belonged there.

"I recognized your signature on the damn note you wrote Karen. Same distinctive letter 'M', as when you signed the drink order at dinner." Cid's voice was void of emotional projections or overreaction. "Your sandwich confirms my suspicions. You ordered a ham sandwich from room service while you were in Karen's suite, right?"

"I don't deny I was there. I don't even mind talking with the authorities. The only hard part is telling you why I needed to see Karen." Mimi waited a moment knowing she had not said enough. "Without complete honesty you will never know who I really am."

Cid sipped some beer. "When you're ready." She answered without judgement. Already Mimi was more familiar to her than most people Cid had known for years. She knew that beneath Mimi's humor and gentleness was someone honest and stable. She had even seen through her air of secrecy and detected a measure of need.

They sat together not feeling the need to speak. The tenderness Cid felt was filled with respectful tact, not one of her normal personality traits.

"When will the investigation be over," Mimi asked.

Each investigation had a pace all of its own, Cid knew. Some were of quick solution. Others gathered momentum as secrets became public knowledge and lies unfolded to expose betrayers. "Could be months or years, if the killer isn't found."

"That long?"

Finishing her Heineken, Cid placed the empty on the table and wiped her mouth with the back of her hand. "Unless the killer makes a mistake or turns out to be a wacko. Confesses up front. Then it'll be over quickly."

Mimi's voice took on the tone of surprise. "Does that happen often? Someone just confesses?"

"No. Just the opposite. Everyone is always innocent. Ask any scumbag on death row. You get an exception every now and then, but it's usually only the fruitcakes that confess. I had a case, ten, maybe twelve years ago. It was never prosecuted, but it probably was the grizzliest scene I've ever come across, and the circumstances surrounding the confession and death were bazaar."

She looked at Mimi, wiping her hands on her Dockers. "I arrived at the murder shortly after an ambulance. Whole front of the house was lit up red and blue. Patrol and reporters were crawling all over the place. A middle-aged housewife, Agnes Doyal, got tired of tap dancing for her overbearing husband, Vernon. She was a sweet old woman, looked like Granny Clampet on the *Beverly Hillbilly's*. And she had motive. Vernon was a heavy drinker, used her as his punching bag. Finally fed up, she walloped him in the back of the head with a fry pan. One of those old-fashioned, black steel jobs. Split his skull from stem to stern. If Agnes had stopped there, she probably could have pled spousal abuse and gotten off with a light sentence, maybe even probation. But she whacked off the bastard's dick and fed it to her dog, Ginger."

Mimi's face whitened, but she didn't ask Cid to stop. She took a hefty swig of her beer. "And the dog ate it?"

71

"Bon appetite. Agnes was a good cook and no one appreciated her culinary talents more than her black lab. Much to the dismay of my male counterparts, she even made sure every cop in hearing range had her doggie recipe."

Mimi pushed her sandwich to the side and then her face took on a look of chilly amusement. "Poor dog."

"Oh, that wasn't the end of it." Cid allowed her voice to trail off as she signaled for another round of beer. "Agnes fed body parts to the lab for better than two weeks. One night it was mushrooms, peas and gravy with an arm, next night cream of celery soup over roast leg." Cid crammed another bite of hamburger in her mouth as if the story was making her hungry. "Then one warm morning, poor Agnes found Ginger dead in the back yard. Called the police whooping and hollering how Vernon had killed her dog. In truth, Agnes had left the remains of old Vernon in the garage and he'd turned a little rancid. The dog died of food poisoning. Agnes never quite understood what she'd done wrong. Last I heard she was still up in Napa at the state hospital, workin' in the kitchen."

Mimi sat up and eyed Cid. "That's not really a true story."

Cid raised her right hand and smiled. "Still have the recipes if you're interested."

Snickering, Mimi snuggled into Cid's arms again. "Don't tell me anymore cop stories, real or imagined."

Cid pushed the rest of her hamburger in her mouth and shoved her plate to the side just as the German waitress delivered another round of beer.

After several moments of silent reflection Mimi spoke, her voice soft. "Wouldn't you know, I'd find you, my own dream come true, and I'm under suspicion for murdering one of my dear friends. On one hand, the hours since boarding ship seem like a surreal nightmare, and, on the other, a fairy tale and we're waiting for happily ever after to begin."

Mimi nestled closer. "Does it scare you to know I was in Karen's room?"

Cid kissed the top of Mimi's head. "No. Should it?"

Mimi shrugged, her shoulders barely moving. "We could avoid talking about Karen's murder, but like you said, your friend Tally wants answers and I suspect you do too." She looked at Cid with silent respect. "I don't want you to have to ask if I was involved; it would shatter something new and wonderful inside of me if you did."

She gave Cid a reflective look, remembering. "Karen was alive when I left her. We had an intense conversation. It wasn't an argument, just pent-up frustration. Karen could be so pig-headed, so dedicated to what she believed right. The details of our conversation pertained to our past. Something I'm ashamed of, but I can assure you it had nothing to do with her murder." Mimi shut her eyes. All that was left on her face was sadness.

It was the first time Cid thought of Mimi as fragile. She could feel her nerves, her shaking. She took her hand, ran her thumb across the top and down the side of it feeling a small abrasion.

"Ouch." Mimi looked down. She seemed uncertain for a second. "My suitcase has a broken handle. I guess I scratched myself."

Cid nodded, kissing the palm of Mimi's hand. She watched her with unreadable eyes. "Got any idea who would want to take Karen out? Kill her?"

"No." Slowly, Mimi shook her head, her eyes lost in distant memory.

"So why's everyone in your little group so tight- lipped?" Cid asked.

"Fear is a great silencer," Mimi said, as if explaining to herself. "Whenever I imagined talking about this, I always hoped it would be with someone like you."

The words now came easy, as if she had wanted to say them for a long time. "Anna had radar for the wounded. She had a certain charm and energy and knew just when to move in and what to do to make us her disciples."

"She was your lover?"

A single bead of perspiration leaked through Mimi's thick makeup and rested just above her right eyebrow. "For a brief time. Anna wasn't into long-term relationships. She liked the high of new love, especially from a sexual standpoint. Bringing a woman out, teaching her the joys of woman-to-woman love made her feel powerful. I don't think she was capable of really loving someone. She had an uncanny instinct for the weaknesses of others and drew her passion from that control."

"And she's dead now?"

Mimi shook her head. When she turned she seemed different. Vulnerable. "North of Seattle, Anna jumped off a bridge." A catch in her voice. "No corpse. The currents are horrible at Deception Pass. Lots of eddies. The police told us the body would probably never be found and callously added that the crabs were voracious eaters in spring."

"Yum. And to think crab salad was on the menu tonight," Cid said flippantly, realizing too late her cop humor was not appreciated.

"It was a terrible time," Mimi continued, her voice thin.

A strange blackness nagged at Cid's heart as instincts and gut feelings tried to push to the surface. "Why'd Anna kill herself?"

Lifting her beer, Mimi drank deeply. It was a gesture indicating her final acceptance that the past was about to be exposed. "In the early seventies I worked as a high-priced call girl. A thousand, two thousand dollars a night." She stopped saw Cid's face fill with surprise.

"All of us. Marjorie, Cimarron, Karen and Claire. Anna's little stable of whores." Tight as a spring, Mimi continued, "Anna's family were the St. Amands of Alaskan oil fame. Her father died on an oilrig when she was six, but her mother made sure she grew up surrounded only by the rich and well appointed. Then, during Anna's last year of medical school, her mother abruptly sold the family business. She sent her cash to a Swiss bank account, packed up her gigolo and departed for Europe. Anna was left high and dry."

"So big-hearted mama provides a good education for her daughter, and then skips out figuring the daughter can make it on her own?" Cid asked coolly.

"Exactly, except there was no love lost there. Anna was glad to see her mother go. What she missed was the money."

Mimi's face dropped. "But Anna was clever. She knew how to use our fears and vulnerabilities to bring in the currency. She recruited each of us carefully. We were all attractive, came from poor and needed money to finish college. We each had been her lover, however briefly, and we all trusted her. Anna was a star-bright, sophisticated and ever so reassuring. What she proposed to us seemed logical. For tax purposes and to protect us from the police, we were considered an elite secretarial service."

Pausing, Mimi looked at Cid as if searching for understanding. "Anna's friends weren't common 'Johns' seeking lurid sex. They were Seattle's older elite and were willing to pay a lot of money for an afternoon or evening of entertainment. Anna made it easy. We worked the weekends and sometimes an evening during the week. She paid our tuition and living expenses and kept whatever else we earned for herself."

"And I'll bet Madame Anna made a bundle from your young bodies with her rich and well-placed friends."

"Yes, the mother cat and her five blind mice. After three years of our hard labor she was once again a very wealthy woman."

Her worried look disappeared, replaced by the blank cop glare that Cid used when she did not wish her thoughts known. "Why'd you stay?"

Mimi fell quiet for a time. A trace of resentment crossed her face. "Anna knew just what buttons to push. Mine was my mother. She raised me alone without the benefit of education. And, melodrama aside, Mama really did scrub floors for a living. Her proudest day was when I was accepted at the University of Washington. She had no idea of the cost…it would have killed her if she had known how I was paying the bills."

Cid again took Mimi's hand. When her fingers trembled she tightened her grip. "So Anna was blackmailing you? Stay and earn the bacon or I'll call mama and tell her you're a scarlet woman. Nice friend."

"In retrospect, Anna was more than self-absorbed." Mimi added her voice carrying a trace of sadness.

Cid was silent for the moment.

As if to reassure herself, Mimi continued, "This was a job. A means to pay for my education." Her mind seemed to wander for a minute. She felt Cid's hand stroke her fingers. "When I think back I feel like a bystander watching a very sad old movie."

"You still haven't told me why Anna took a swan dive."

Mimi's expression was now a mix of torment and fear. "You've heard of Senator Pierce Lawton?"

"Yup. Fat senior senator from Maryland. A congressional icon with Kennedy status and a pork barrel heart. Died in a rafting accident a number of years back. Your neck of the woods if I recall correctly."

Cid looked at the butt of her cigar with an obscure expression. "Columbia river. Authorities dredged the water for weeks. Raft and supplies were recovered. Never found the stiff."

All at once, Mimi's shoulder's slumped. "It was a cover-up. The senator was on a rafting trip, but had decided to spend the evening on a short excursion into Seattle. I wasn't privy to how all the pieces were put in place, but I do know Senator Lawton died in our house, sprawled across Marjorie's and my body."

Visibly shaken, Cid seemed poised to ask a question, then did not.

"Lawton was an idiot. A sloppy drunk who pinched nipples and patted rear ends as if it were his God-given right." Mimi touched her chest. Her voice rose in sudden anger. "He ripped Anna's blouse. I can still hear the ping of little pearl buttons bouncing off the walls and the floor. And then he pulled Anna down and forced her legs apart. When he released her wrists to tug at her slacks, she shot him. Anna never allowed men to touch her. Especially blubbering old fools who couldn't even maintain an erection unless they were violent."

Mimi regarded Cid for a moment, caught between the relief of disclosure and the horrible realization of the act.

"Where'd the gun come from?"

"Before he ran for political office, Pierce Lawton was a county sheriff. He never got out of the habit of carrying a gun. His pants were lying on the floor, holster still clipped to the belt and waistband. The gun was only inches from Anna's hand."

"Why didn't you try and stop her?" Cid asked.

Mimi stared at her for a moment, her expression was an odd combination of satisfaction and regret. "I've asked myself that a thousand times over the years. It all happened so fast." Her voice was edged with contempt, "And he was such a bastard, somehow it seemed just."

"And the body?"

"Someone came late in the night and took it away. I never knew who, but I got the sense the senator's aides were involved. Esteemed senators don't die in bordellos. The cover-up seems ironic now, after the Clinton, Lewinsky mess."

With a hint of wounded puzzlement, Mimi continued. "Anna swore us all to secrecy. Said we were accomplices to murder. If one hung, we all hung."

Abruptly a picture of the noose lying next to Karen Phelps' body flashed before Cid. "Where was Karen and the rest when all this was going on?"

"Karen had just returned from the hospital. She'd recently finished her internship and had planned on moving out in a matter of days. When Anna protested Karen's decision to move, Karen had dismissed her behavior as overbearing and proceeded with her plans to pack that evening. Claire had just shown a banker pal of Anna's out the front door."

Mimi's voice was flat, "Cimarron was alone in her room downstairs. They all came running when they heard the shots."

A sudden jumble of aged images leaped into Mimi's mind. "It was horrible. The senator's wrinkled face with his dead brown eyes still holding a stare of disbelief."

Listening, Cid narrowed her eyes. "Why no police?"

"I was twenty-one, dearie, scared out of my mind. I'd just seen a man shot dead. I made my living as a whore. What chance did I, or any of us for that matter, have with the police."

There was something nasty in Mimi's eyes, a darker quality. "We were all aware that we were participants in a crime, Anna made sure of that. Took pictures. Even Karen looked bad. She came in the room and immediately went to the senator's aid. Started CPR. The gun lay on the bed next to the senator. The pictures looked as if Karen were kissing him after he had been shot."

As Cid leaned back she could see how uncertain Mimi still was. "More blackmail?"

"Yes. Three days later Karen broke into the safe in Anna's bedroom and took her parcel of cash, nearly $300,000. She also found the black book that contained our clients' names, including the senator's, and the pictures taken the night of the murder. She hid it all somewhere and then told Anna she was going to the police. That afternoon, several people witnessed Anna's body hurling through space when she jumped off the bridge at Deception Pass. She planned well. If the fall didn't kill her, she would drown. She couldn't swim. The 'star' was dead and we were left with the guilt."

Two women walked past, engrossed in conversation. Cid was silent until they were out of earshot. Her eyes cut back to Mimi. "And then?"

Mimi shut her eyes. The memory breaking through the darkness. She almost whispered, "We all had a meeting and decided that with Anna's death, justice had been served. There was no point in going to the police and ruining all of our lives."

"What about the senator?"

"We figured it was better his family believe he drowned in a rafting accident, than drunk in a whore's bed. Besides, a cover-up had already been set in place by his people. Who were we to argue with big shots?"

Cid stared at Mimi quieted by astonishment. "One hell of a story. Whatever happened to the pictures and loot?"

Mimi gripped her stomach as if nausea had overtaken her. "Karen was supposed to destroy everything, the book and the pictures. The money was given to a woman's shelter anonymously."

Cid gave a low whistle. "And let me guess, outta the blue the pictures and little black book suddenly reappeared."

"Yes." Mimi gazed at her hands and then met Cid's intense stare. "Karen was a tortured woman. No matter how much of her income she donated to scholarship funds, she couldn't get past the fact that she had worked her way through medical school by lying on her back. As the years passed, she became both judge and jury. She wanted Anna to pay for the past even in death. Late last year she called the scandal sheet, *Probe,* and anonymously told them she had proof Anna St. Amand had murdered Senator Pierce Lawton."

"Holy shit. I never heard anything about that."

Mimi gave a rueful shake of the head. "Thankfully Karen called me before she did anything more. I was able to appeal to her reasoning, told her the decision to expose facts surrounding Senator Lawton's death was one that had to be made by all of us. She had called *Probe* from a pay phone and never left her name. When she didn't call the paper back, I suspect they wrote her call off as some crackpot seeking attention and never pursued the matter. Karen then arranged the reunion cruise and agreed to bring the black book and pictures with her."

Cid looked at her for another moment and then her gaze grew distant. "And how the hell did you feel about that?"

"I thought she was wrong to be dredging up the past." Quite deliberately, Mimi met Cid's eyes. "I've spent a lonely life living with the regret of Anna's mistakes and the errors of my youthful sexual choices. What good would full disclosure serve now? That's what Karen and I heatedly discussed in her suite and in the end she agreed that we all should meet and make a joint decision to destroy the black book and pictures. The meeting was going to take place tonight after dinner."

Cid sat back, law enforcement guidelines and compassion warring in her head. For nearly thirty years, Anna's crime had scarred Mimi's life. All that Cid clearly knew was that Mimi had paid a high price for someone else's hideous act. "Where are the book and pictures now?"

"Last I saw them they were lying on Karen's bed."

The bartender, a bubbly Hispanic in her late twenties, announced a line dance. A crowd of would-be participants surged toward the tiny dance floor laughing.

As she watched the happy group, there was a tightening in Mimi's throat. "Why did this happen? Why did Karen have to die? Despite her bitterness she was good. She didn't want anyone hurt. She was just searching for peace after feeling so helpless for so many years." Tears gathered in the corners of her eyes.

Cid wondered how many times she had heard those exact words. How many times she had wanted to escape tear-filled eyes at a bloody death scene. She had never found an answer. Never knew how to help those left behind, how to take away the anger, the helplessness, the fear.

She pulled Mimi closer, got a whiff of her flowery perfume. "Just saying you didn't kill Karen is enough for me, but it sure as hell ain't gonna pacify Tally."

Mimi sensed something unspoken. "I take things in quietly. Most people don't realize I'm watching or paying attention. Maybe it's just an instinct, but I seem to know what people are thinking, at least when it pertains to me. Why is it you trust me and your friend Tally doesn't?"

Slowly Cid extracted a Virginia Slim from the pocket of her white shirt, held it in her fingers for a second and then placed it, unlit, in the ashtray. She flipped a palm back and forth.

"Hell, right now Tally's not out to make friends. She wants to crack this case. She'll take a slim lead and ram it up a suspect's ass if she thinks it'll get her somewhere."

Cid spoke in matter-of-fact tones. "A criminal investigation is a search. In her eyes, you're prime, and before she's done she'll have stripped you and your pals buck-naked. She's a clever cop, very fair, but if your story doesn't wash she'll nail your butt six different ways."

"Are you going to tell Tally what I just told you?" Mimi asked cautiously.

"Yep." Cid again picked up her cigarette. "Besides," she said a little louder than necessary, "you are a killer."

It was a curious remark, Mimi exhaled, shook her head, stung. "A killer?"

"Sure...you stopped my heart the moment I laid eyes on you."

When Cid's smile finally registered, Mimi gave her an ironic look. "If your heart stopped over a little innocent flirting," there was humor in Mimi's voice again, "what's going to happen when you get laid tonight?"

****

No Corpse

She stood in the bathroom for a long time just looking at herself in the mirror. Time passed. How much she didn't know.

Mimi opened her purse, reached for her makeup, and saw the black book and pictures. She drew her breath in sharply.

12

Sunday, July 12
12:49 a.m.

The Old Piano Room was small. A dozen tables, black in color, the inside walls awash in blue light with lush silhouettes of a sax and trumpet player. On the opposite side of the room, a bay window overlooked the water. The effect was both startling and elegant. It was the kind of club that attracted jazz connoisseurs or lovers who wanted their words intensified by atmosphere.

A vintage pianist with pasty gray hair skillfully danced his fingers across white keys, filling the room with soft jazz. The only thing missing, Tally noted, was a haze of smoke and Ella hanging tightly to a microphone, the mellowness of her velvety voice reaching out.

For the first time since viewing Karen Phelps' body, Tally felt a wave of enjoyment. It would not last long.

Two middle-aged women sat in one corner, sipping what appeared to be strawberry daiquiris. Marjorie Temple was seated at a long table on the opposite side of the cozy bar, nursing a white wine, and was accompanied by Katie. Crossing the room, Tally looked from Marjorie to Katie, showing her surprise at finding them together.

Katie jumped to her feet nearly spilling her wine and put her arms around Tally, holding her close. "I've missed you."

Gently, Tally took Katie's face in her hands. For a brief moment her pulse quickened. Their foreheads touched. Aware people were watching, their kiss was light, but not without feeling. She felt places inside warm, wanted to give Katie attention and tenderness, but felt the tug of Marjorie's eyes.

"I called the room several times," Tally's voice softened, "I was worried about you."

"Aye, and I noticed you'd been to our cabin when I changed my clothes." Katie spun around, head thrown back, hair flying, showing off a new sundress, the same soft blue as her eyes.

"The suitcases were a mess, Tally McGinnis, a near hurricane. I thought I'd trained you better." She winked.

Tally felt a twinge of fear, gazed at the tables around them and then gently pulled Katie in the direction of a huge potted palm that afforded them a small amount of privacy. "I haven't been back to our cabin."

Katie's look was surprised. "There's no mistakin' it; someone was in our suitcases." Her eyes were widely fixed on Tally.

"Could be as simple as a nosey cabin steward," Tally paused, drew in one sharp breath, "or it could be a warning."

She held Katie closer, working hard to conceal her alarm. A set of master keys, Cid had said, was missing from the Haitian woman's cabin.

A tremor moved through Katie's body. "Should I be frightened?"

"Cautious." Tally searched Katie's face. "From now on we stay together."

"I could think of worse things," Katie answered mischievously touching her fingers to Tally's lips.

They looked at each other and fell briefly silent. Tally glanced at Marjorie and then back at Katie. "She's beautiful isn't she?" Katie whispered.

Tally nodded.

"Hmmm. And are you thinking she's more beautiful than I am?"

"Absolutely not!" Tally answered immediately, giving Katie's rear end an affectionate pat.

"Smart woman, Tally McGinnis, you really know what's good for you." They laughed and hugged.

Katie became quiet for a moment, pressed herself tightly against Tally. "There's something sad about her, don't you think?" she whispered with regret.

Watching Marjorie's profile, Tally nodded, "Beautiful, successful and so alone." What, she wondered, had happened to make this lovely woman so miserable. It made Tally sorry that she didn't know Marjorie in some other context.

"And," Katie continued her face expressing a deeper level of concern, "she's nervous about something. She's returned to her cabin at least twice since changing clothes. There's something not right, Tal."

"Perhaps, it's time we have a look in her cabin," Tally whispered nuzzling Katie's ear.

Katie's expression mixed query with surprise. She pressed her head against Tally's. "You mean we're 'gonna toss her room?'"

Tally cracked a smile. "You've been watching too many cop shows." When she was truly amused, Tally's grin was genuine and infectious. She kissed Katie's forehead.

"Surely, Tally McGinnis, you're not thinking Marjorie might have something to do with her friend's murder? Her tongue may be tart, but I'm sure her heart is good."

Tally's soft features rearranged themselves into a sensitive, yet penetrating stare. "I hope you're right."

"Marjorie and I have been having ourselves a time in the casino. Losing our money of course." Katie scanned Tally's face more closely; in that moment, Tally saw her understand Marjorie Temple was indeed a suspect in the murder of Karen Phelps. Katie's fingers slid across Tally's cheek. It was as if the silent gesture helped her digest the truth.

For another moment Tally leaned against Katie, their touching was sensual and content. She kissed Katie's hair and felt the vibrations of warmth flutter away as Mimi and Cid nosily ambled to the table.

In a resonant voice, Cid called to a waitress, "Two Glenlivet's neat."

Mimi flopped on a black, bench seat, the cushion making a swooshing sound. Cid gave her arm an affectionate squeeze and then walked over to Tally and Katie, an unlit cigarette protruding from her lips.

Cid's expression was one of apprehension. "Listen up." She paused for a moment as if preparing herself.

Part of Cid, Tally realized seemed shaken. For reasons she couldn't explain Tally wanted to reach out and hold her. Instead, she picked up a pack of Sea Pearl matches from a vacant table and lit Cid's cigarette. Her silent simple gesture seemed to center Cid, calm her.

Slowly Cid recounted everything Mimi had told her.
The story cut to the bone.

For a moment Tally felt bewildered and then sorrow surged through her. "Prostitution?"

"Same set up as Heide Fleiss; poor little rich girl and her cast of needy call girls. Anna cooked the books to her benefit, murdered a senator and left a trail of scars," Cid added.

Except for the dim lights near the piano, the room was cast in dark shadows. Tally could not read Mimi's face. "How sad." She glanced at Katie and then back at Cid. "You believe Mimi's story?"

"Hell yes! She had nothing to gain by telling me her tale and everything to lose. Anna was a dumb-ass piece of garbage."

"Unless Mimi's twisting the facts to her benefit." Tally waited a moment. "Anyone can say just about anything about the dead and not get an argument."

They glared at each other, eyes locked, both unwilling to yield an inch of ground. Their friendship would survive this, they knew. Their friendship wasn't at issue. It was their wills that were in conflict.

Cid stopped, red anger touching her face. "The bitch killed herself, Tal, because she was about to get nailed for the murder of a United States senator."

"Which brings up another point. Pierce Lawton was a powerful man." Tally shook her head, "Don't you think it a little strange that his staff would assist in the cover-up of his death?"

"No. This ain't the first politician to get caught with his pants down and have his ass covered by his faithful companions. Think JFK. Protecting a politician's image is part of the D.C. scene."

Cid's voice was thick with confidence. "Lawton was a good ole boy. Flew a little close to the ground and didn't watch out for mountains, but he had powerful friends. Ran with the likes of Lyndon Johnson before he was president and a few other skirt chasers. Kept a girl in one hand and a bottle of Jack Daniel's in the other. Like Lady Bird Johnson, Gwen Lawton was an obedient politician's wife. You're too young to remember, but both women were loved and respected...maybe even pitied because they were married to high-wheeling slimy bastards. I suspect Lawton's staff would have covered up his death out of respect for Gwen Lawton if nothing else."

As best she could, Cid was trying to put a positive slant on Mimi's story. Tally found this both touching and painful. "Okay, for now I'll buy that, but then you've got to tell me why Karen Phelps is dead."

"She had the black book and the pictures."

"Right. But according to Mimi's story, the pictures were Anna's safety net. If the rest of the college chums, a.k.a. working girls, were innocent of Senator Lawton's death, the exposure of the pictures and the little black book would be detrimental to all of them, including Karen. Phelps' appeared to be a well-adjusted successful doctor. Why would she call a scandal sheet and offer up evidence that could possibly incriminate her? And why would she wait twenty, nearly thirty years to finally expose Lawton's killer? Doesn't add up, Cid. And, more importantly, it doesn't explain why she was killed or who killed her."

For the first time, Cid gazed at Mimi. Her eyes were distant, wounded.

"Mimi said the last time she saw the black book and pictures they were lying on the bed in Karen's suite?" Tally asked.

Cid nodded.

"And now they're gone." Tally lowered her gaze, her inference obvious. "How did Mimi seem when you talked with her?"

"Scared, ashamed, little sad." Cid answered her temper tightening.

"Was she twitchy? Did she seem nervous at all? You pick up anything?" Tally said her words slowly and in a less accusatory way.

"No!" Cid answered emphatically with a breath of smoke, the anger in her eyes fading. "But she did refer to Anna as a star several times."

Tally stared at her, the importance of what she was hearing growing in her mind.

"A star?" Katie asked looking at Tally.

"An area of flesh in the form of a star was carved in Karen Phelps' buttock after she was killed." Tally answered quietly.

The terrible image of someone taking pleasure from such an act hung in the air as the faint sound of conversation drifted toward them.

"How evil." Katie hesitated. "Who do you think killed her?"

"Right now, I could make a pretty good case that one of them," Tally pointed at the table, "is the killer. With Karen out of the way, the black book and pictures gone, their past is history. Their reputations restored. The question is, which of our college sweethearts had more to lose?"

"Aye or gain." Katie's tone grew quiet. "You're forgetting the money. If the black book and pictures survived all these years, wouldn't you be thinking, Tally McGinnis, that maybe the money never made it to the woman's shelter?"

Tally cocked her head, distractedly pushing her fingers through her bangs, more red than strawberry in the dark room. The possible money connection had never occurred to her. She smiled at Katie. "Cid what do you think?"

Cid took two long drags on her cigarette before squishing the butt into the soft soil surrounding the potted palm. Her gaze mingled worry and deep thought.

"Possible. But if you're gonna throw out theories, then you have to consider Anna as the prime perp." She stopped, seemed to warm to the idea the longer she thought.

"Anna had motive, opportunity and a lotta years to work up a good hate. She'd also murdered before. And don't forget she was a doctor, could have cut that little star in a nanosecond."

Tally's eyes narrowed. "There were witnesses. People saw Anna's body falling from the bridge."

"The hell." Cid chided. She straightened as if gathering strength. "I got the impression this Deception Pass ain't no little plunge, so witnesses would have been a ways off. They saw a body falling from the bridge. No corpse, remember? Coulda been any damn stiff."

Tally's gaze seemed to turn inward as if she weren't listening. It was a gesture, not of rejection, but of deep thought. She drew an exasperated breath. "The world already believes Anna's dead. If she's not, why would she come back and risk exposure? I'd be more inclined to believe Mimi took the black book and pictures, and, if the money does still exist, maybe that too. Until I learn differently, Mimi was the last one to see Karen alive and the only thing that supports her story is her word and right now I'm not sure what her word is worth."

In the dark shadows Cid's face looked tight, her jaw muscles flexing. At that moment, Tally saw the years of loneliness fall away from Cid's eyes, the stubborn strength evaporate as she looked at Mimi.

"Give her a break, Tal. She made bad choices a long time ago, but that doesn't make her a liar or change her goodness." Cid's face seemed unspeakably sad.

Silent, Tally turned the book of matches in her hand as if gauging the weight, then slowly tossed them on the vacant table. She felt the complex ripple of her own emotions-fatigue, fear for her friend, anger at the college chums, admiration of Cid's loyalty.

Cid turned to her, fingertips touching her arm. Tally wanted to help her by speaking to her heart, but knew she could only help by acting like a good detective.

"Do me a favor, Tal. If you ever plan on killing someone, don't do it on my vacation. And don't murder anyone remotely connected to my lover."

"I'll keep that in mind," Tally answered with a lazy grin.

13

Sunday, July 12
1:04 a.m.

Tally had her cop face on now, eyes intense, taking in every nuance, every breath of air. She pondered all the known facts in the Phelps homicide and couldn't see anything simple and obvious she had missed. She knew the case probably hinged on the relationship of the dead woman and her old college roommates. She also knew she was going to have to cultivate a certain trust with the surviving women if she was going to get anywhere, especially working on such a limited time line.

Close to regal in appearance, Marjorie's faultless taste was reflected in the perfectly cut black Versace pantsuit she now wore. She shifted so there was room for Tally and Katie at the table, the wine in her glass coming precariously close to the rim as the table was jostled. Beneath Marjorie's icy air of self-interest was, Tally felt, another feeling, perhaps fear.

Seated, they inspected each other. Marjorie suddenly presented a sarcastic grin, displaying a mouthful of teeth to good to be true and a voice honed razor-sharp.

"Cimarron gathered the troops, but forgot to show up herself. How typical."

"Easy, Marjorie," Mimi said with the fatigue of pointless redundancy.

"This whole business with Karen has made my nerves raw, and I'm weary beyond belief." Marjorie sighed and then appraised Tally, gave her a coquettish smile. "At dinner this evening I was lead to believe you were an extraordinary detective. Left no rock unturned. This ship is only so big, surely for someone of your reputation, one measly little killer can be found. Karen deserves better. If it were a matter of money I certainly would be willing to pony up a fair amount--say enough to have you double your efforts without involving us."

Beneath the table, Katie's fingertips grazed Tally's knee. It distracted Tally just long enough to keep her anger at bay. Though soft, her words were biting, "I'm not for sale. And, sorry to say, you're involved whether you like it or not."

Marjorie looked up, pushed herself forward to demonstrate her persistence, stared directly into Tally's face, and resumed talking, her voice sharper and more contemptuous.

"I don't see you as authority. And I believe by legal standards we're entitled to an attorney before we are questioned." She waved her hand with arrogance. "If you're not willing to work for us, you need to understand, I not only find this little meeting an inconvenience, but an invasion of my privacy and my legal rights. Besides, I don't kiss and tell. Especially to perfect strangers who probably have no respect for the truth."

"Truth? What the hell do you know about truth?" Cimarron asked, gulping Budweiser and nosily sliding a chair to the end of the table before taking a seat. "Our little cold-hearted Marjorie looks out only for herself."

"Nice of you to join us. I see, as usual, you dressed for the occasion," Marjorie fired back.

"My God, will this rivalry never end?" Mimi asked severely. "I don't care what secrets our past holds. I don't care whether we like each other or not. Karen is dead. Show some respect!"

The table remained tense. The only difference was a certain courtesy, punctuated by a nod or a glance.

Silent, Tally watched. They were an unlikely group. For reasons she still didn't understand she found each one suspicious. Yet all in all, she had already learned more than she had expected. Each woman wore identical rings on their right hands-one large clear-cut diamond set in a simple gold band. Whoever bought the rings had good taste, knew how to spend. She wondered which one of the rings, if any, had been responsible for the indentation left in Karen Phelps' neck.

Tally pointed at Mimi's hand. "Nice ring."

For a moment Mimi said nothing, slowly turning the ring on her finger. Finally she answered, "A gift from Anna the day before she died. People like Anna prey on the worst in us. I came from poor, never had a diamond before. She would have known I was too greedy to toss the ring away."

In profile, Marjorie froze. Then her left hand moved across her right covering her own ring.

Slowly Tally pulled her notepad from her back pocket, her voice stripped of benevolence. "You're correct, Marjorie, I'm not the police as you know it," she began with forced patience, "but it won't do any good thumbing your nose at me. Let's just keep this friendly, say I'm asking for your opinion regarding Karen's untimely death."

Tally looked at the threesome. "After all," she said, the voice of reason, "you knew Karen best. Occasionally, after a shocking event like this, friends or family may recall important details when their minds have had a chance to settle. Something from the past perhaps, something that may clarify why someone would want to kill Karen."

Marjorie's eyes flashed with discontent. She pressed a hand to her chest, as if she were having a sudden attack of angina. "Karen and our past with her are private."

"Sorry," Tally said in a matter-of-fact voice, "no such thing as privacy in a murder investigation. Was Karen having trouble with someone? Someone on the shady side of the law? Maybe a past John?"

Marjorie's head snapped up. She shot a querying look at Cimarron, then her eyes bore into Mimi's. "You lonely fool, what all have you told them?"

Mimi looked away, her gaze following two women nuzzling each other.

Cid's expression was a mixture of interest and soft caring, as if to help get Mimi through this.

"Knowing our pathetic Mimi as I do," Marjorie snapped, "I would guess she has filled you in on everything from bygone days. Character assassination is one of her more formidable attributes."

Marjorie drummed her fingers and gave Tally a sidelong glance. The smile that followed seemed bitter and filled with denial. "Beware, detective, of the possibility of lies. In Mimi's twisted solitary world, recollection is sometimes blurred-even filled with pitiful apparition. Unless of course all you're interested in are the lurid details of a delusional mind."

"If this is a contest to see who can be the most nauseating, I declare you the winner," Cid said, eyes glinting with an arrogance of their own. "It's easy to imagine you nude with a dead senator in your lap."

"I have nothing further to add," Marjorie answered quickly, her obvious shame having done nothing to snatch the sarcasm from her tone.

"You at a loss for words," Cimarron said swilling the last of her beer, "that would be a first." Her southwestern twang seemed lost in the game of one-upmanship.

Tally searched Cimarron's face, a little steel in her voice. "Why don't you tell us why you were in Seattle recently, Cimarron. I'm sure it wasn't just to take in Expo 2000 with Mimi." She watched the calculation in Cimarron's eyes. Watched her determine what to say and how much spin to put on it.

Cimarron folded her arms. "I went to Seattle to pick up my cruise ticket." She laid her hand on the table, the diamond and gold glint of her ring dancing in the dim light.

"The mail wasn't good enough? You had to fly from New Mexico to Seattle to pick up tickets?" Tally asked incredulously.

Cimarron now seemed to have the caution of a protective mother. She looked at Marjorie, then Mimi an edge to her monotone. "We wanted the reunion to be special. Figured the trip needed our plannin'."

Sensing something important left unsaid; Tally was silent for the moment, trying hard not to read too much into Cimarron's stray comment.

Mimi looked pale and at length said, "We all got a letter inviting us on the cruise."

Tally leaned forward. "And?"

"The message was a simple invitation with tickets enclosed. Mine had a blank prescription from Karen's office mixed in with the paper. Naturally, since Karen had planned everything, I assumed the letter was from her and the prescription accidentally included. She claimed she hadn't sent the letter nor had she bought the tickets. It was the signature..." Mimi's words trailed away, the reticence of fear. "You see, dearie, the letter was signed by Anna."

There was a long silence and then Mimi continued in a trembling voice, "Cimarron came to Seattle at my request. I was scared, so was Claire. We all had received the same letter and a blank prescription from Karen's pad."

She looked from Cid to Tally. "Cimarron convinced us Anna's signature was a hoax. The only thing that made sense was Karen had written the letter to heighten the drama surrounding the pictures and black book."

"Why?" Tally asked.

"That was one of the things I intended to find out when I saw Karen in her cabin today, but she adamantly denied writing the letter." Mimi's eyes traveled back to Cid. "She actually trembled when we discussed it and had no idea how someone could have gotten a hold of her prescription pad."

Mimi's head bent forward. Her hands touched her face as if in shock. "She claimed to have gotten the same letter."

"Then who the hell wrote it?" Cid asked her voice brittle.

"I don't know," Mimi's voice went cold, "and I don't know who killed Karen. Anna knew exactly how to exploit us when she was alive and now she's somehow reaching out from the grave hurting us again." The simple words carried the anguish of lives wasted and years of emotional baggage.

With thoughts of Karen fresh in their minds, Tally threw a curve ball, abruptly asking, "Who was Ceta?"

The question seemed to revive the fear Cimarron displayed earlier and then her fear became another expression-anger.

"Marjorie's right. This little get-together is a big inconvenience." Her blue eyes turned nearly black. She pushed back from the table, stood and slowly lumbered from the bar not bothering to look back.

Cid placed a fingertip on the rim of the ashtray. "Now there's somebody with something to hide."

"You must understand," Mimi defended, "we were victims. Some of us moved beyond our past, others still harbor the pain."

Tally watched Cimarron leave, her mind moving in too many directions at once. She was beginning to understand the players, but had the uneasy feeling she might be missing the obvious. She stared at Marjorie. "Who was Ceta?"

"I never heard of her." Marjorie's lips formed an indifferent smile.

Cid looked at her with undisguised dislike. "Right, and cows fly."

Tally gave Marjorie an interested, more personal look. She was insecure and neurotic. In Tally's experience, such people lied habitually. "Talk to me now or I would suspect in the next few hours you'll face someone from the international law community."

Tally kept her face bland, bluffing with steely resolve. "More to the point, given this ship is of Panamanian registry, any questioning, in all likelihood, will fall under the jurisdiction of that country. Now that's an inconvenience you should consider. South American law enforcement has been known to use a less than hospitable approach when gathering information regarding a crime. And I can assure you they don't have a clue what the words due process mean."

Her voice was clear, determined, "And then, of course, there's the publicity. I'm sure *Bon Ton* magazine would be thrilled to have it known that their fashion editor was under investigation for murder."

"She's right," Cid added leaning back. "Every hot-shit narc and promotion-driven cop is gonna ream your ass." She was enjoying watching Marjorie squirm. "And you can bet the media will be at the dock the moment this ship sets anchor."

They became a unit, a practiced team of one mind determined to keep Marjorie off balance. It was an old cop trick that both Cid and

Tally knew well. Hit suspects from every angle with no logical sequence until you get the information you need.

In the stricken silence, Tally turned to Marjorie. Saw her on the edge, knew she was ready to break.

"The first time someone kills, it's scary. Unnerving. But afterwards, after they've succeeded, it becomes business. Maybe even fun. If you aren't going to cooperate, I sure as hell would watch my back."

Marjorie jerked her head up, an alarmed animal smelling danger. "Ceta was nothing special, just our housekeeper in Seattle."

Tally's expression turned confused. "In college?" She looked at Cid. The time line was wrong, it didn't fit with the youthful appearance of the corpse in the cooler.

Mimi reached across the table and touched Marjorie's hand. A momentary spasm of sadness crossed Mimi's face. Her eyes dropped to the table. "She lived with us for nearly four years. Ceta was a secretive woman, hardly ever spoke with us. She and Anna were close, not lovers, more like conspirators. They even resembled each other."

She paused, looked up, watched a few more women enter the bar. "She moved out the day before Anna died. Took her little girl, Sabra. We never heard from her again. I always thought that strange, but then, that was probably part of Anna's plan." She felt the warmth of Cid's leg against hers.

Tally leaned over her arm nearly touching Mimi, subtly crowding her space. "How old would Ceta be now?"

Mimi looked from Cid to Tally with a humorless smile. "Ceta was eighteen when she came to our house...she was pregnant...she would be in her late forties now." Her hand moved to her purse as if checking to make sure it was still in her lap.

"And the little girl...her age?"

Mimi's voice and gaze were steady now. "Late twenties, maybe thirty."

"And the child was Haitian?" Tally asked.

Mimi looked past Tally, out the window as clouds filled up the sky and rain began to beat down on the deck. She was desperately trying to get her thoughts in order.

"Yes. I haven't seen her since she was a small child." For a moment she was silent. "Sabra was always big for her age. Beautiful dark skin. Her father was Caucasian, an American. Worked at a pizza pub just off campus where Ceta had washed dishes. She was Cimirron's little protégé. It nearly broke her heart when Ceta took her away."

"Is that why Cimarron left when I mentioned Ceta's name?" Tally asked.

Mimi bit her lip, the turbulence of memory clouding her eyes. "I would imagine that's partly the issue, although Cimarron and Sabra have been reunited by mail for years. Cimmaron's real problem is superstition. Ceta, as well as Anna's, religion of choice was voodoo. In fact, they both were manbo's or mama's, voodoo priests. Cimarron has never been able to get past Hollywood's version of voodoo. Rather than a religion practiced by thousands, Cimarron sees voodoo as witchcraft and believes Ceta placed a curse on her after Anna died."

Mimi lowered her head. When she looked up her eyes were filled with painful candor. "It doesn't matter, dearie, how silly or dramatic that all sounds. For Cimarron she sees Ceta as a sorceress responsible for her financial failings."

"Cimarron's got money trouble?" Cid asked surprised.

Mimi breathed in, "Yes. She's been hemorrhaging money for years. All her savings. She even sold off a hundred acres of land. Combine the low price of beef and competition with the large conglomerate ranches, she hasn't made a profit in five years and is on the verge of losing the remainder of her acreage and her homestead."

In a neutral tone, Tally asked, "You are all successful women, probably even a little competitive with each other. Why would Cimarron tell you she was on the verge of bankruptcy?"

Mimi looked into Tally's face. "When Cimarron came to Seattle she wanted to borrow $150,000." Her voice filled with sorrow, "I would have given it to her in a second, but I don't have that kind of money."

"And what of the $300,000 that never made it to the women's shelter?" Katie asked bravely.

Instinctively, Marjorie sat up straight, her eyes widened slightly, signaling surprise, but she said nothing.

Mimi shrugged, looking first to Katie then to Tally. "I don't know anything about that."

"Who," Tally pursued, "supposedly delivered the money to the woman's shelter?"

"Karen." Mimi stared at Tally fixedly. "Like I said, I don't know anything about that."

Tally placed the small gold charm on the table. "And this?"

Marjorie gasped. "That's Anna's caduceus!"

Shock came to Mimi's face, then tears touched her eyes. "Anna gave that to Sabra on her third birthday, made her promise never to take it off." Mimi drew a breath, staring at them, while her long tapered fingers played with the strap on her purse.

The Glenlivet arrived. Mimi turned to the waitress as if pleased by the interruption. The glass was a magnet for her shaky hands. She raised the amber liquid to her lips and drank deeply. A shiver seemed to move through her body.

"Outside of Anna, Claire knew Ceta best. If you want more information, you'll need to speak with her."

Eyes narrowed, Cid looked around. "Where is Claire?"

Marjorie shrugged, flopped her hair. "When we were summoned to this inquisition by Cimarron, she mentioned that she couldn't find Claire. She left a note on her door." She looked to Katie for conformation.

Katie hesitated and then nodded her head.

"Claire probably has turned in for the night, frail thing that she is," Marjorie said folding her hands displaying perfectly manicured fingers. "Let her rest."

Instantly Tally felt an unsettling ping in her gut. Her eyes bore into Mimi's. "What's Claire's room number?"

Mimi frowned, as if struggling to remember. "Starfish deck, room 423."

Tally looked at Cid and said, quietly but firmly, "Get Vincenzo."

14

Sunday, July 12
1:31 a.m.

The faint wobble of rough seas and a persistent scent of rain from a brewing tropical storm created the sleepy illusion of being gently rocked as Katie and Tally rushed down the red-carpeted corridor of the Starfish deck.

Some weary travelers had retired for the evening, most still frolicked on upper decks, unwilling to give up even a moment of excitement.

Tally's stomach double-clutched when she thought of Claire Taylor. She feared the worst and somehow felt responsible for not having solved the riddle of Karen Phelps' death before someone else was possibly hurt.

With one hand Tally clung to Katie's arm and with the other tapped lightly on the door to cabin 423. The note from Cimarron was still tucked tightly in the corner of the door just above the handle.

When no one answered, she knocked louder and then inserted her security card, stabbing in the code Vincenzo had given her earlier in the evening. The door swung open to a small room with two twin beds, a tiny closet and bath. The furnishings were less decorative than functional. There was no sign of a struggle and no sign of Claire Taylor. Tally's posture suggested relief.

"Where could she be?" Katie asked with concern.

"Bingo. Late show." Tally's expression was speculative as they stepped inside the cabin. "Claire didn't appear to be a party girl. Maybe she stayed at the buffet or caught a late movie."

As if on cue, Vincenzo Pallino appeared. "Scusa, scusa," he pleaded, hands moving rapidly, face pinched and scowling. In the half-light of the hallway he looked like a busboy delivering an order.

"The library," he gasped in Tally's ear. "She's been dead awhile."

Tally's eyes widened. In a second her senses sharpened and her heart gave an intensified thump. "Claire?"

"Si." Vincenzo heard the elevator and looked down the hall. "Cidney is waiting, we must go at once."

In a quick succession of moves, Tally grabbed Katie's hand and was out the door. Vincenzo tried to keep pace, his ponderous gait and heavy breathing was that of a man who had never exercised much and was now showing the effect.

The late cabaret show had just ended and suddenly the halls were crowded. Knots of passengers drifted past, laughing and talking, oblivious of any trouble. Tally dodged shoulders and nearly knocked over a maintenance worker sweeping spilled peanuts.

Her heart jumped into her throat when they arrived at the library, her eyes glassy with dread. Curiously she noted that the area around the library was quiet. Not many vacationers spent the first night of their cruise perusing books.

While Vincenzo unlocked the huge mahogany door, Katie stepped to the side, took a seat on a brown leather couch and squared her shoulders. "I'll be waiting here, Tally McGinnis, no need for me to see what awaits you in there."

Tally gave her an uneasy nod. The fine hair rose up on the back of her neck and, with it, the anxious feeling of being watched. When she spun around, the hall was empty.

Conscious of Tally's distress, Katie reached out and touched her arm adding, "I'll be just fine, you'll be but a few feet away if I need you."

The remark, Tally sensed, carried an unspoken determination. When Katie had made up her mind, there was no reasoning. Though bone-weary, she found new energy in Katie's touch. She again nodded and followed the chief of security into the library.

A small, portable room divider had been pushed in front of the window to block the view of any would-be voyeur. Tally heard her own sharp intake of breath when Cid's hand touched her shoulder. She managed a nod, but said nothing as she looked around the room.

The polished wood floors bespoke elegance. The tops of the teak tables orderly, as books had been neatly returned to their proper places on the selves. There were a couple of paintings on one wall of the Sea Pearl's sister ship, the Sea Lion, and a large world map on another.

Sitting in the semi-dark, almost in a corner, was a beautiful charting table. Tally saw the large red glasses first. They lay on the floor crushed and twisted. Claire Taylor sat at the table, her head resting on her arms, as if taking a nap. Tally walked to her.

A rope hangman's noose lay on the table. The atmosphere was so hot a glint of perspiration had already formed on Tally's forehead as she carefully took in the scene.

"Who found her?" Tally asked evenly.

Frowning, Vincenzo stepped forward. "Maintenance crew."

Claire's face was turned to the side. A thin purple line ringed the dead woman's neck. A trickle of blood had seeped onto her white cardigan sweater leaving a pattern that resembled a Rorschach test. Her tiny fingers rested innocently across the pages of a book titled, *Caribbean Folklore,* a perfectly cut star of flesh removed from the back of her left hand.

Slowly Cid crossed the room and stood next to Tally. "See the eyes?" She angled her head toward the dead woman.

Tally moved closer, bent and looked into the white, frail face. She made herself concentrate even though she felt a piercing agony. "My God, the eyeballs are gone." She swayed backward struggling to make sense of what she saw.

A surprising shaft of light illuminated the room when Vincenzo flicked on a row of fluorescent lamps. The light served to intensify the dark bloodied sockets that had once held Claire Taylor's intelligent brown eyes.

The room was stifling. "Can we get the air on?" Tally asked wiping her flushed face with her hand.

"Si." Vincenzo Pallino walked across the room to a thermostat, rubbing his souring stomach. His eyes were darkly ringed. His body sagged.

Watching the chief of security, Tally was struck by how fragile Vincenzo Pallino looked. How deflated from the cheerful figure she had met only hours earlier.

"Been dead a while. Three, four hours." Cid said in a practical tone. "And no damn struggle again. No bruises or rough treatment. Hell, looks like she didn't even lose her place in her book." Her eyes deftly roamed the room.

Tally pushed her bangs off her forehead. "Maybe someone had the draw on her. You know, held a gun to her head. No one is that timid when their life is threatened. It's a natural reaction to fight. Unless of course she knew the killer and didn't see what was coming."

Briefly, Tally glanced at Cid. She knew Claire Taylor had suffered as her life's breath had been cut off. The physical pain would have been filled with terror and panic. The mental anguish inconceivable. The MO was the same as the Phelps' murder, only this time there were no rope contusions on Claire Taylor's wrists. Whoever killed her had simply overpowered the thin frail librarian.

Tally's eyes were cold now. "Mimi was alone while you were with Vincenzo. She would have had plenty of time to pull this off."

Tally gave Cid a quick knowing glance. "Katie also mentioned Marjorie was out of sight for awhile and who the hell knows what was occupying Cimarron's time."

"But which one is capable of murder?" Cid asked, her face expectant, as though waiting for Tally to pursue this line of thought.

Instead, Tally declared, "It's a reconstructed crime scene. She's posed like Karen Phelps."

"Posed?" Cid shifted her weight heavily.

There was a pattern here, she was sure. "The clues left at the scene are only those that the killer intended to be found. Think about Phelps' hands, her fingers in particular."

Tally inhaled reaching past her weariness for patience. She knew Cid would listen until she reached her own conclusion. "Had her hands not been prominently displayed we never would have noticed her broken fingers."

"Your point?"

"Same thing with Claire Taylor. Not only were her glasses crushed and twisted." Tally could feel Vincenzo watching them. "If her head hadn't been turned to the side, posed, none of us would have noticed the empty eye sockets. There's no mess. No blood. No butchery. The perp isn't trying to shock us. There's a message here," she continued with quiet vehemence.

Cid's face contorted with interest. "Go on."

"Karen Phelps was a doctor, primarily a surgeon. Her fingers were violently broken. And Claire was a librarian and her eyes were removed. Our killer, in some after-death ritual, destroyed both of their careers."

"Interesting theory." Cid's tone signaled a hard- earned knowledge that the act of murder could often be broad and perplexing. "You're thinking this was all planned?" She asked her face expectant.

"Flawlessly." Tally retorted. "A vengeful mind at work long before this ship ever set sail. An impulse killer would probably have been seen leaving Phelps' cabin or the library. Things wouldn't have been left so clean, so orderly. I'd bet if some unsuspecting fellow traveler strolled into the library tonight, they didn't even notice Claire Taylor was dead."

"But why, how you say, such an elaborate plan?" Vincenzo asked moving to Cid's side, his thick physique staining his T-shirt.

Cid gave a thin smile. "Answer that and we'll nab this asshole."

Tally stared deeply and silently at Claire Taylor. How had this frail, innocent appearing woman ended up here?

"Has anyone called her family or, more importantly her lover, Candice?"

"No," Vincenzo answered with a slightly contemptuous air. His eyes followed Tally's to the dead woman's body. "Shipmaster Cruises will handle notification at the appropriate time."

Tally's voice hardened, "And if this were your wife or your sister, what would you deem the appropriate time?"

Vincenzo considered this and then shamefully lowered his eyes. "Procedura, Signorina."

Tally stared past him. "I wonder who could hate enough to cut out someone's eyes?"

They stood in silence each harboring their own thoughts, their own terrible torment.

Finally Tally forced herself to look at Claire more closely. The killer's work showed on the dead woman's face. Burst vessels, mouth open as if gasping for breath, drool caked and crusted on her chin. Her hands were nearly translucent as they rested on the colorful pages of the book. Suddenly Tally stabbed the table with her forefinger. "No ring."

Cid's blue eyes looked down at the thin fingers. Earlier she noticed the gathering of white raw skin at the knuckle of Claire Taylor's right middle finger.

"And no blood," Tally said with a probing look. "Ring was removed postmortem. I'd bet the same for Phelps."

Cid seemed to consider this, pulled her lighter and cigarettes from her shirt pocket, looked at the 'No Smoking' sign and lit up anyway. She blew out a long heavy stream of smoke. "Phelps' body was buck naked. No jewelry."

The statement reminded Tally, although she did not need it, of how vigilant Cid was when viewing a victim.

Vincenzo mopped his forehead with his handkerchief. An awkward moment passed. "Perhaps the ring was of great value to someone--maybe just a common thief."

"That's fucking brilliant, Vinny," Cid answered, her voice registering impatience as a blast of smoke filtered out her nose.

"Common thieves don't break fingers and cut out eyes. Shit," she muttered in frustration, "No perp. No motive. Missing pictures.

Missing black book. Missing rings. It all points to a woman who's supposedly been dead for nearly thirty years."

Looking at Cid with curiosity, Tally felt her own confusion closing in. She knew the answer to the puzzle was somewhere in the facts she had already gathered, but couldn't sort through it.

She was still now, her emerald eyes riveted on Claire Taylor, looking, searching. Slowly, Tally bent, settling on her knees, her finger pointing at the dead woman's lap.

"Ask yourself this, why was the bookmark left on Karen Phelps' thigh?" she looked from Cid to Vincenzo, the detective in her alert.

Curious, Cid hunched forward, hands pressing on her knees, her face taking on a red tinge as she gasped for breath. "What the hell is it?"

"A mouse."

"You mean a damned rat?" Cid stumbled back nearly falling, her face now blood red.

Vigorously, Vincenzo shook his head. "No rats on Shipmaster..."

"A computer mouse," Tally interrupted her nerve ends vibrating. For a moment she imagined the killer carefully placing the plastic form in the dead woman's lap. "Add it up. Tickets sent with a blank doctor's prescription from Karen Phelps' office--Phelps's dies. Then a bookmark with the initial's C.T.--Taylor dies. And now a computer mouse. The perp has left us a chain of tip-offs, each clue connected to the next victim's occupation."

Cid's bushy eyebrows jerked upwards. "Holy shit, Mimi's the next hit."

Tally felt a tightness in the pit of her stomach. Suddenly the puzzle pieces were starting to form a picture. She raised her voice for emphasis, "That would be the obvious, unless she's the killer and is trying to deflect some of the heat."

Cid studied Tally with smoldering eyes, then glanced at Vincenzo. "I'll be with Mimi." Her tone held both fear and urgency as she headed for the door.

For a moment, Tally's eyes closed. She wondered for whom she felt worse-Claire Taylor or Cid.

Abruptly, she stood. "Wait." Her voice softened. "Where does Marjorie fit in this? She's certainly got the arrogance and the smarts to be the mastermind. I just don't see her with blood on her hands."

"Marjorie's a loser...couldn't pick a winner in a one- horse race." Cid answered stubbornly, her thoughts elsewhere.

"What I'm saying is this: Maybe someone like Cimarron is her foot soldier." Tally walked over to a shelf and ran her finger along a line of books as if she were looking for something. "Cimarron is big and strong. She easily could have taken down Phelps and Taylor."

Cid shook her head. Flicked her ashes into the palm of her hand. The anger in her eyes receding. "Doesn't fit. Cimarron can't stand the bitch. She sure as hell isn't gonna be her patsy."

Tally shrugged. "I want to have a look in Marjorie's room. Can you and Mimi keep her busy, say, for the next thirty minutes?"

"Jesus." Cid gave her an exasperated glance. "Thirty minutes max! If I have to listen to that woman any longer, I may be the one to end up in jail."

Tally smiled and added jauntily, "Take Katie with you. She somehow has managed to find some redeeming qualities in Marjorie." Her eyes narrowed. "Keep an eye on Katie, Cid. Someone was in our cabin earlier."

Cid took another drag on her cigarette trying to sort out the confusion she felt. The sound she emitted was part, grunt, part hiss.

Tally dropped her head. When she looked up Cid was gone. She drew a breath and faced Vincenzo. "Ever read anything by Ferber?" she pointed at the bookshelves.

Vincenzo seemed surprised by the question. The fluorescent lights gave the room a bluish cast, accentuating the dark circles under his eyes. "Magnifico! Classics. *Giant, Show Boat.* Splendido!"

"How about *Cimarron*?"

Vincenzo pondered for a second, his expression mildly curious. "No. It's, how you say, a good read?"

"Can't remember," Tally hesitated, "at least most of it. There's not a copy on board by any chance."

Vincenzo eyed the bookshelves. "Our selection is limited."

Tally was not sure where she was going with this line of questioning. Maybe it was just instinct, but something was rattling around in her head that needed an answer.

"Your office," she said at last, "I need to call San Francisco."

He studied her curiously. "Si."

"You've also got several 9mm in a locked case. I want one."

Vincenzo began pacing. His face was filled with tension, but his body drooped with fatigue. "The captain would not...think of the passengers...Shipmaster Cruises would not..."

"Fuck Shipmaster Cruises." Tally said impatiently. "Three people are dead. I don't intend on being the fourth. I want a 9mm and I want it now!"

15

Sunday, July 12
2:12 a.m.

She watched from the fringe as the huge crowd from the bingo bonanza surged into the halls and stairwells. She had cut the cable wire in her pocket exactly three feet in length, long enough to encircle her victim's neck and still leave leverage for the kill.

She saw Tally's strawberry blond head and began to follow at a safe, discrete distance. Her hands trembled with excitement.

16

Sunday, July 12
2:20 a.m.

The warm tropical rain spattered the porthole and the intense thump of the Sea Pearl's huge engines beat with a heart rhythm as Tally stood just inside Vincenzo Pallino's office. A 9mm Glock rested comfortably in the small of her back, her green Izod shirt hanging loosely around her waist to conceal the gun. Vincenzo, along with his two security guards, had retreated to the library to remove Claire Taylor's body.

Eyes grainy from fatigue, Tally pressed the phone against her ear. Between the hiccups of static she heard the intermittent bleep from her mother's cell phone. It was nearly 10:30 California time, and she guessed her mother would be curled in bed with a good book.

The call was picked up on the fourth ring.

True to her fiery red hair, Victoria McGinnis deferred to no one and could be either officious or downright playful. She wore little makeup on her lovely skin and was always, even when in bed, impeccably layered in lacy ruffles and dangling jewels.

"Tally darling, how lovely to hear from you. Harry rang not ten minutes ago and said you would be calling. How I envy your vacation, sweetheart. All those exquisite jewels for sale on the islands. You will bring me home a trinket or two, won't you darling?"

The line buzzed and cracked. Tally had the familiar sense that conversation with her mother was, at times, its own mystery. "Of course, Mother."

"Is everything all right? Harry mentioned there was some trouble on board ship. Nothing to do with you or Katie, I trust?"

"No, Mother, we're fine. I just need some information. I know you've read Edna Ferber's *Cimarron*. Can you tell me something about the story."

"Certainly. It's a wonderful tale of Oklahoma and the Cravat family. Yancey and beautiful, strong Sabra."

Silent, Tally felt her suspicion move to fact. She closed her eyes, let the silence stretch until her mother finally said, "Do you need more? That wasn't much of a depiction. Are you sure there's nothing wrong, darling?"

"No, Mother, you've been a tremendous help. I'll call you again tomorrow and I promise to scour the jewelry shops until I find you the perfect gift."

Tally hung up and waited, her mind drifting back to Claire Taylor. She never heard the door open.

The heavy metal handle of a gun glanced off the side of Tally's head. Pain shot across her face and down her jaw. White flashed through her vision. She hit the floor hard.

And then the lamp cord was around her throat. She couldn't breath, her eyes were exploding, her brain fading black.

She would not give up this easily. She raised her arm, bringing her right elbow up and then down with ferocious intensity, finding her attacker's ribs. There was a scream.
The shadowy form behind Tally lurched back clutching her side.

With her last bit of sense Tally pulled at the wire. It came loose in her hands. She sucked in air. Her temples throbbed as blood rushed back to her brain.

The gun again met its target, coming down hard across Tally's right shoulder. She cried out. For a second everything froze. Then she scrambled to her knees. Frantically attempted a leg sweep as she grabbed for the edge of Vincenzo's desk. Her shoulder burned with pain as she pulled herself upright, spun quickly and executed a perfect front kick. The kick did not find its intended mark, the room was empty.

Running on pure adrenaline, Tally whipped out the Glock, checked the fifteen-round magazine and slammed it back in place. She thought again of how her attacker had already killed three good people and silently moved out the door, 9mm leveled.

The recessed light just outside Vincenzo's office had been broken; the hall was cast in dark shadows. The crunch of glass echoed from under her loafers. Tally stopped, stood motionless, listening and peering.

She had no way of knowing which way her attacker had fled until she heard glass breaking behind the engine room door.

Moving in a crouch, she slowly opened the door. More darkness. The bellowing engines were so loud, Tally reflectively lurched back, as if pushed by the noise. She kept listening, trying to still her heavy breathing. As her eyes adjusted to the darkness, she moved through the door and dropped to one knee.

After a few seconds, she stood, walked to the right keeping her foot in contact with the steel wall. Two minutes passed. Then five. She was fairly certain the killer had to come past her to escape. She waited. Tried to hear anything. See anything.

A light, far in the distance, suddenly blinked on. Shadows became huge piston's moving rhythmically up and down. How stupid. Of course there would be more than one door to the engine room.

Two crewmen chattered with each other in a tongue foreign to Tally. She saw them round a corner pointing at broken lights. Then another movement. A familiar dark figurer darting across the room.

A bullet ricocheted off the heavy steel. Tally dove to the left. The two crewmen let out a loud squeal. A shot whined between them and smacked the doorframe. They hunched down and ran.

Shoulder rolling across the floor, Tally leveled her gun. Another bullet, fired blindly, pinged off the steel wall just to her right. She saw the muzzle flash and inched her way forward, the adrenaline pumping.

"Give it up, Cimarron, it's over."

"Just go away, leave me alone."

"So you can kill someone else?" Rising from the floor, Tally scooted forward hiding behind a large metal toolbox.

"I didn't kill anyone."

"Really? I've got a nice bloody bruise around my neck that says otherwise."

"I wasn't tryin' to kill you. Just used a little lamp cord. Thought maybe if I scared you, you'd back off...leave us alone. Let things go."

"And your gun? Is that a scare tactic too?"

"No. I brought it for me, figured if things didn't work out the way I'd hoped..." Cimarron's voice trailed away.

"Your credibility sucks, Cimarron. You expect me to believe you haven't killed anyone, yet every time I move you shoot."

Cimarron shifted her clammy hand around her gun. "You're forgettin' I own a ranch. Lots of undesirable critters around. Hell, I shot the rattles off a snake one day just for fun. If I'd intended to hit you, we wouldn't be havin' this conversation."

"You've been stalking me."

"No way. I told you, I just wanted to be left alone."

"It's not that easy, Cimarron. You're going down for at least two murders. Karen Phelps and Claire Taylor."

"Claire's dead?"

Tally leaned forward, then lunged for the wall that separated her from Cimarron. She peered around the corner, breathing hard, windpipe raw. "Your little innocent act isn't very appealing."

Another shot rang out, hit a drum of oil to the right. A slick brown flow instantly spread across the floor.

Tally's head snapped back pressed hard against the cold steel. She had gotten a good look at Cimarron's gun. A thirty-eight, six shots, four already spent.

"I told you I didn't kill anyone." The shock of disbelief pulled at her face. "God, not Claire...I just wanted the money." Cimarron's voice now had the jittery tone of someone slipping over the edge.

"So, Katie was right, the $300,000 never made it to the women's shelter?" Tally's grip tightened on the Glock.

Cimarron laughed, a low gargling sound. "Back in those days, Karen was no philanthropist. Oh, she hated how the money had been earned all right, but she sure as hell wasn't givin' it away."

"The two of you were in cahoots?" Tally asked lowering herself to the floor.

This time Cimarron's laugh was hollow. Her voice held bitterness. "Sweet and righteous Karen had no intentions of sharin' the money. She didn't want nor need a partner. For my silence, she offered me a fifth of the loot, a little over $50,000--the down payment on my ranch."

"So," Tally said, "for thirty years you kept your mouth shut, bilked the others out of their rightful share?"

Cimarron seemed to ponder this. "Yes," she answered at length, the voice of a survivor. "Greed, even for a country girl, is a powerful motivator."

"And you never told the others about the money?" Tally asked surveying the room.

"No."

Tally paused a little for effect. "And now you're desperate for money again and you've become a motivated murderer."

"No." Cimarron's gun clanked against a metal railing, as if to drive home her point. "I was desperate, but not that desperate. After I put the heat on Karen, told her I was gonna spill the beans about the money, she came around, said for years she'd wanted to make things right with Mimi, Marjorie and Claire. Hell, it was just a matter of finding the right way to do it. That's what the cruise was all about. She was indebted. Karen's practice was successful. She'd made a ton of money over the years and as she'd gotten older, she felt guilty for cheatin' her friends. That's why I sent the wine. I wasn't askin' her to forgive me...I was tellin' Karen we all would forgive her."

Cimarron's voice suddenly took on a new and deeper desperation. "You can try everythin', includin' prayer, but you ain't gonna hang these murders on me. I didn't need to kill anyone. Once Mimi got her money I knew she would loan it to me. With nearly thirty years of interest added to the principle, my debt worries would have been over."

Tally shifted uncomfortably. There was something in Cimarron's voice that made her words ring true. "Who else knew Karen was repaying the money?"

Hesitation. "No one."

"If you didn't kill Karen and Claire, who did?"

"I don't know."

"And what about Sabra?"

"Sabra?" Cimmaron voice now carried both surprise and fear. The past was all catching up with her. She was shaking hard as she forced herself to speak.

"Sabra lives in Haiti. Works for a voodoo manbo. I wrote her just after the cruise was planned. Told her all about it. Told her how close I would be to her home and how I wished I could see her." More fear. "She's all right, isn't she? I love her. She always been my little girl. I named her you know. Sabra Brooks."

As Tally listened she remembered an earlier conversation. A little butterfly tattoo, Cid had said, with the initials SS on her breast.

"Sabra's last name was Brooks?" Tally asked inching forward, trying to get a clear view of Cimarron.

"Yes. I gave her my name. Her father was a prick. A slimy bastard who wouldn't own up to his parentage."

For a surreal second, Tally blocked out everything: Cimarron's voice, engine noise, the oil that touched her pant leg. With mounting apprehension she asked, "What was Anna's last name?"

"St. Amand. Anna St. Amand."

It took Tally several seconds to process what she had heard. Voodoo manbo. A little butterfly tattoo with initials SS. Sabra St. Amand.

"Did you tell Sabra about the money?"

"Of course. She wants to live with me. I never could afford to send for her before. I told her after I got straightened around financially she could finally come. She was downright excited. She is all right?"

Tally didn't answer, instead she reached in her pocket, pulled out several quarters and threw them across the room. The clatter created her intended results. Cimarron fired. One bullet left.

"Is Ceta in Haiti?" Tally asked with slow deliberation. She could see Cimarron's face now. Her eyes were small and cold and she paced nervously. Her gun pointed at the ground. Her glances darting.

"Don't know. Sabra wouldn't talk about her mother. Ceta didn't care two hoots about her. I never understood why she took her away from me." She seemed to forget Tally was there. Contempt crept into her voice. "It was me who loved that child. All I ever wanted was my little ranch and Sabra as my daughter."

She lowered her eyes, seemed to be weighing her thoughts. When Cimarron finally spoke her voice was filled with sorrow and disillusion.

"Sabra's dead, isn't she? That's why you're asking all these crazy questions. She's gone and so's the money." She looked down, seemed to weigh the effect of deceit. "What a shame we can't go back and undo our mistakes."

Tally had barely slept in the last thirty-six hours and had eaten little. Maybe that combination caused her reflexes to erode when Vincenzo Pallino burst through the engine room door, Luger trained on Cimarron.

"Freeze!" He shouted, his thick Italian accent lost in the moment.

Tally managed to scream, "No-o-o-o!" But it all happened fast.

By instinct, more than anything, Cimarron raised her gun.

In one quick motion, Vincenzo let loose with a volley of bullets, the 9mm chattering as each shot found its target.

The smell of gunfire filled the room.

Cimarron rose up in slow motion, spun around and slammed back against the blood-spattered wall before sliding to her knees. Her mouth went slack and dropped open and her eyes held the gray tinge of death before her face hit the floor.

The chief of security may have lacked backbone and instinct, but he was a crack shot.

Tally took off in a crouch, threading her way across the engine room.

She turned Cimarron over. A half a dozen slugs had removed most of her left side. She had bled-out in seconds. The frozen look on her face was pure surprise.

Cimarron could have been thinking about her dead friends when she raised the thirty-eight to defend herself, but Tally guessed her last thoughts were more to do with striving and failing-trying to put difficult memories to sleep, only to find out the past never rests.

"The killer. Yes?" Vincenzo looked miserable, shaking his head slowly, the Luger held loosely at his side.

"No." Tally watched the chief of security's shoulders sag further.

"It was self-defense," she answered, the words partially sticking in her throat. She looked back at the motionless body. She wondered if she would have been so quick to fire had she been in Vincenzo's shoes: she knew at once the answer was yes.

"I'll speak with Shipmaster Cruises on your behalf if you like. There shouldn't be any charges brought against you."

He hesitated for a moment, looked down at the dead women, gazed at her shiny cowboy boots and bright yellow shirt. "Fuck Shipmaster Cruises."

The captain arrived minutes later, followed by the purser and the doctor carrying yet another body bag.

Questions were asked, notes taken, the body finally removed. The captain shuffled his feet a lot. Seemed to feel the weight of a brewing scandal for ShipMaster. Tally and Vincenzo remained silent when he announced the ship would return to the United States at daybreak.

17

Sunday, July 12
4:46 a.m.

Two hours later, Tally was wearing the battle scars from Cimarron's attack. A blue bruise on the side of her face and a shoulder that only worked with immense effort.

She leaned against the wall outside Marjorie Temple's cabin trying to absorb all that had happened. Less than a day had passed since five vibrant women had boarded the Sea Pearl. Now three, along with a young Haitian, were dead. She felt a sadness wash over her as she tapped lightly on the door and waited. Glancing around, she stepped forward, slipped in her security card and punched the code.

Slowly the door opened.

She heard the sound of Celine Dion singing, "My Heart will Go On" and expected Marjorie to round the corner at any second. Tally waited and then flicked the light switch.

The cabin was larger than Claire Taylor's. Brightly painted. A queen-size bed. Two dressers and a table the size of a birdbath. In the corner the bar was open. A can of Diet Pepsi sat next to the sink.

Slowly, Tally crossed the room. She was alone.

Edgy, she quickly sifted through the closet. It was crammed with clothes. Versace, Armani, Ralph Lauren. Everything to keep the fashion editor's impeccable image in tack. The belongings said a lot about Marjorie Temple.

Next she scoured the dressers. Under the bed. The bathroom. She realized, as she searched, that both careers and reputations were at stake and felt a twinge of guilt when she found nothing.

With disappointment, Tally turned, surveyed the room one last time. It was then she saw Marjorie's luggage stacked in the corner. Three Andiamo leather suitcases and a large green canvas bag with Nike stenciled on the side.

Tally could imagine Marjorie parading through airports and hotel lobbies with her Andiamo accessories, but never a canvas bag with a Nike logo.

She felt a chill on her skin as she picked up the heavy bag. A tiny brass lock held the zipper in place, but she could feel the outline of small, elongated packets and knew she had found Karen Phelps' pilfered booty. The question was, what was the money doing in Marjorie Temple's cabin?

Tally heard the door click. Startled, she heaved the bag atop the suitcases and dove to the side, behind the bed.

Instantly the scent of Marjorie Temples' perfume filled the room.

There were footsteps, someone moving across the room, a faint scrapping sound and then the door opened and closed. When Tally looked up the Nike bag was gone.

The air-conditioning system hummed vibrantly as Tally yanked open the door and scanned the hall. Barely five minutes later she was standing on the Sea View deck watching the waning storm clouds drift. The sun, at water's edge, slowly ascended from sleep. She took in a deep breath trying to clear her mind. Trying to understand.

When she turned, she wasn't surprised to discover the glint of a white busboy uniform in the shadows. Anna was taller than she had expected, six feet or better. She was trim, youthful in appearance, her long black hair thick with waves. And even now, there was a dignity about her.

"Stars don't usually come out at sunrise." Arms folded, Tally leaned back. The wind whipped her strawberry bangs. "But then star isn't a true depiction of you, is it? Sicko is a better fit or maybe just stone-cold killer. Was the money really worth it?"

"Yes," Anna's voice was subtly refined, yet lacked warmth. "I've lived in near poverty for over twenty years. It was my turn to know luxury again. I sacrificed both my career and my life for those women. They owed me."

Anna twisted a length of cabled wire around her hands and pulled it taunt. The sun reflecting off the amber ring she wore.

"I don't think so." Tally's eyebrows rose in disbelief, unimpressed with Anna's air of egotism. "On your behalf, Karen and Claire may have been obliged to enter a self defense plea regarding Pierce Lawton, but they owed you nothing more. It was your own warped instincts and greed that created your problems."

Tally gazed at the wire, dropped her arms and slowly slid her hand to the small of her back.

"You set yourself up to fry when you killed Ceta." She stared into Anna's black eyes. "I'll give you this much; you did your homework, researched the currents at Deception Pass and knew her body probably wouldn't be found. I'd guess you dressed her in your clothes and either killed her or knocked her out before you dumped her over the bridge. And you and Ceta resembled each other...just enough, so you could use her passport and slip away to Haiti undetected. The child was good cover, gave you a certain credibility. What I don't get is why you killed Sabra."

Anna's eyes glinted with cold hatred. "Excess baggage. She was ungrateful as a child, seemed to always resent me as she grew older. She wanted to move to the states and live with Cimarron. Sabra never would have kept my secret and eventually she would have figured out that it was me who killed her mother. " She snapped the wire and took a step forward.

Once more Tally was struck by Anna St. Amand's intense selfishness. She kept a careful eye on her, watched her every move. "So, Sabra was your pawn. She got you onboard by disguising herself as a man and then she became dispensable?"

Anna shrugged. Let out a low laugh. Took another step forward. "Sabra was dumb like her mother and she never loved me like she did Cimarron. I owed her nothing and now, once you're gone, there's no proof I didn't die at Deception Pass."

This time, Tally laughed. She brought the Glock into view, leveled it at Anna's chest. "Get a grip on reality. I'm going to be sitting in the front row when a jury finds you guilty of murder."

"I'll never go to jail. Never!"

Anna unwrapped the cable from her left hand, whirled, and whipped the wire at the Glock.

Tally let out a muted groan and felt the warmth of blood on her wrist as she drew a bead on Anna and fired.

Anna reached for her shoulder, came up with a handful of blood. "You fucking cunt."

She swung the wire wildly, fell forward against the railing as if embracing it. Turning, Anna crouched snapping the cable at Tally's legs, catching khaki. She clamped her wounded arm against her chest and in a vain attempt to escape suddenly leaped over the rail, teetering on a ledge a little more than four feet wide. She grabbed an iron girder and clung on for dear life, the left shoulder of her white busboy uniform now stained crimson.

Tally jumped to the side, the images of Karen Phelps and Claire Taylor lurking in her mind as she again took aim. There was something primal inside that made her want to empty her clip.

"Anna?" Mimi's voice was nearly lost in her own disbelief.

Stepping forward, Cid touched Tally's shoulder. "It's over, Tal. She's not going anywhere unless she wants to take a header for real this time."

Breathing hard, Tally looked into the black of Anna's eyes and saw only evilness. It took several long seconds before she lowered her gun.

Katie scrambled out of the doorway, folded Tally in her arms and squeezed. "Are you okay?"

All at once, Tally felt calm. "Yes."

Puffy white clouds raced across the morning sky. The smell of the sea and the first blush of humidity descended on the ship.

Marjorie joined Mimi, Nike bag hanging from her shoulder like a very large, expensive purse. Her face was red and perspiration gathered above her lip. They regarded Anna without expression. Only their cold glare betrayed their emotion.

At length, Marjorie raised her hand, pulled the diamond and gold band from her finger. "I wore this all these years because I believed I had somehow let you down. I even believed I was partly responsible for your death." Pain crossed her face. With trembling fingers she hurled the ring at Anna.

"You've got this all wrong." Anna's voice sounded so plaintive, so familiar. The same seductive tones she had used years ago. "I faked my suicide to protect each of you."

Mimi stepped forward, her fists clenched.

"Wait." Anna gave her a cool, appraising look and continued, "It worked, didn't it? You've all got good jobs, made big money. No one knows you whored."

She reached over and pressed on her wounded shoulder, leaning forward across the rail. "And I didn't kill Karen and Claire." She looked at the Nike bag. "It was Cimarron. She was desperate."

Furious, Tally pulled away from Katie. "That's bullshit. You kill people like swatting at flies. It's all a selfish game for you."

"Is it?" Anna asked, her eyes narrow slits focused on Tally. "Seems to me it was Cimarron who had the gun."

Anna looked at Mimi. "Ask your friend here what happened to Cimarron."

Mechanically, Mimi turned.

Tally expelled a breath. "She's dead," she said and then explained why.

Anna smiled, casually dropped the cabled wire over the edge and carefully removed her busboy jacket allowing it to flutter away in the wind. Her wounded shoulder seemed to have stopped bleeding. "Like I said, I'm clean."

"Right." Cid mumbled placing her hand on Mimi's shoulder. "And Jeff Dahmer was a vegetarian."

With half a smile Anna asked, "What have you got on me? Nothing. No fingerprints. No murder weapon. No one saw me leaving the crime scenes." Anna snapped her fingers and smiled again. "I suppose we could weigh the circumstantial evidence, but then there isn't much of that either, is there?"

"There's these." Mimi pulled the black book and pictures from her purse.

Cid glanced at Tally. Mimi lied to me her expression said.

Anna merely shrugged. "Pandora's box. I'm sure the media would find all of that interesting," she said pointing at the book, "but really Mimi, who suffers in the end. If you and Marjorie don't outright lose your jobs...well, I can only guess your work environment would be made less than pleasant."

Anna licked her lips, tapped the metal ledge with the toe of her shoe. "Attitudes have changed in the last twenty some years. The general public is fed up with their political representatives. I believe the actions I took against Senator Lawton would now be viewed as heroic. So that leaves only you and Marjorie as tainted."

She became still, looked squarely at Tally. "You've got nothing on me."

With genuine distaste Tally answered, "You confessed to me."

Anna gave a brief laugh, her voice hostile. "Now why would I confess to something I didn't do? Do you have trouble with the truth, detective? Or are you just trying to find a way to appease the guilt you feel over Cimmaron's death."

The hatred in Anna's eyes showed. "Your word against mine." She let go of the girder, pausing for effect. "And, I'm sure my attorney will advise the jury I am a simple manbo serving the spirits and the people. A woman of compassion and sacrifice, who not only spent the best years of my life raising someone else's child, but a loving soul who opened her heart and ministered to thousands of poor Haitians."

With an invincible smile Anna shrugged. "How very tragic Cimarron was the killer."

Tally stiffened and then allowed herself to relax. "Good try, but you've forgotten Sabra. For Cimarron, very little else mattered...she never would have hurt her."

"Sabra?" Marjorie appeared devastated.

Tally stepped forward, moved closer to Marjorie. "Excess baggage is how I think Anna put it. Sabra was probably the first to die."

The instant Anna's gaze met hers, Marjorie knew Tally was telling the truth.

Anna waved her hand as if trying to move them apart. "Look, there's always been plenty of money for all of us. Let's divvy it up. I'll go my way. You go yours. There's so much more now that Karen and Claire are dead."

In a single agile movement, Marjorie pulled the Nike bag from her shoulder. "You always thought money was value." She raised the heavy bag and threw it to Anna's left just over the rail.

Eyes keyed on green canvas, Anna leaned to the side, wheeled around, trying to catch the bag with her good arm. It was a reflective action and for an instant she was suspended in mid-air. Then gone.

Tally jammed the Glock in her waistband and ran for the rail, tugging at a leathery, white life preserver.

Mimi's voice was quiet, calm. "She can't swim."

"And it must be a four-five-story fall from here." Cid added joining Tally at the railing. "She was dead as soon as she hit the water. The things people do in the name of greed."

Tally shook her head. "We've got to look for her."

"I've already pulled the silent alarm. Crew will be here in seconds." Cid pointed at a red box on the railing. Pausing, she looked into Tally's face. "It'll take thirty, forty minutes to turn the ship and get a rescue boat out. In the unlikelihood Anna survived the plunge, I doubt even she can walk on water that long."

Epilogue

Sunday, July 12

9:00 a.m.

The Sea Pearl's mahogany deck glistened with the arrival of the new day and puddles of dew and salty brine withered on white tabletops as the first blush of heat engulfed the stern of the large vessel.

The sun's ascent from the majestic Caribbean was cathartic. Tally breathed deeply and for a split second the voyage became what it was intended to be, a romantic vacation in an atmosphere of beautiful sun-drenched women.

Curiosity seekers passed their table and stared openly. Gossip had run rampant from the moment the captain had made the announcement that the Sea Pearl would return to homeport due to a terrible misfortune. Although he never elaborated on what mishap had occurred, people assumed he was referring to the poor woman who had fallen overboard.

At the same time, the captain publicly thanked the Phoenix Detective Agency for helping avert an even larger crisis and announced, once in port, passengers would be transferred to the Sea Lion and would continue their vacation without further interruption.

A few people wanted answers to all of their questions, but, for the most part, passengers heard what they wanted to hear and simply allowed the festive party to continue.

Tally sat with her feet propped up on an empty chair, Katie beside her, the warmth of her hand squeezing Tally's.

Cid took a long pull on her Bloody Mary. "How much money you figure was in that Nike bag?"

Leaning back, Tally moved her sunglasses on top of her head. The brash sunlight made her squint. "According to Marjorie, Karen felt compelled to pay a fair amount of interest. I'd guess half a million or better."

Cid's bushy eyebrows shot up. "Hell, that's enough loot to make a person consider taking up deep sea diving." She finished her drink and slid the glass across the table. "Guess it would be a good idea if I learned to swim first."

"And fend off sharks," Katie added tilting her head.

For two hours the crew had searched for Anna St. Amand's body without success. They concluded, in the end, that she had probably died from her fall and her body had drifted with the currents to some final resting place.

At Vincenzo's insistence, Tally had spent the same two hours conferring with the surviving college roommates. Although an official investigation would take place once they returned to the Port of Miami, Tally was fairly certain when she had finished her interrogation that both Marjorie and Mimi were innocent of any involvement in the murders of Karen Phelps and Claire Taylor.

Cid signaled a steward for another drink, lit a cigarette and placed her sandled feet next to Tally's. "How'd our snobby fashion editor end up with all the cash?"

"Karen Phelps gave it to her just after everyone boarded ship. Marjorie was the only one she trusted with money," Tally answered, sliding out of a white windbreaker, exposing a bright yellow T-shirt stenciled with a beautiful angelfish.

"Marjorie was the one person, outside of Karen herself, who had personal wealth. So Karen threw caution aside, told Marjorie about the money and gave it to her for safe keeping."

"Aye," Katie said slapping her knee, "that's why Marjorie was so nervous, kept returning to her room."

"Yes. Karen was so sure Cimarron would try and steal the money she didn't want it in her cabin. And her distrust of Cimarron ran so deep, she unintentionally transferred both her fear and suspicions to Marjorie. That's why there was so much animosity between Cimarron and Marjorie."

Cid looked off in the distance. After a time she said, "Karen was an obvious hit for Anna, she thought she still had the cash. But why the librarian, Claire? She was a complete innocent."

"I can only guess one sin led to another," Tally said her voice carrying a trace of sadness. "Anna wanted everyone from her past eliminated so she could start over. Claire, like the others, was just another inconvenience that needed to be removed."

"And the black book and pictures?" Cid asked starring at the deck.

The clipped sentence, Tally thought, had an undertone of hurt. "I left them with Mimi and Marjorie after the search was over."

Cid frowned. "That's evidence against Anna, Mimi and Marjorie. Pierce Lawton's been dead for a bundle of years, but there ain't know statute on murder. Do the crime, share the time."

Tally pulled her legs down, bent forward, arms resting on her knees. "You can't kill Anna twice. And other than witnessing a crime, both Mimi and Marjorie are innocent of Lawton's death. What regs or laws are going to be served by turning over evidence that will only hurt the guiltless?"

Tally reached out, touched Cid's arm. "I understand some of what you're feeling. Don't judge Mimi too harshly. She was trying to protect people she loved. That's an instinct, not a crime. Best place for the black book and pictures is alongside the Nike bag on the bottom of the ocean."

Cid looked at her for a moment. Then, slowly, shook her head. "This love business is a little more complicated than just jumping in the hay."

Tally leaned back, feeling the sunlight on her face and glanced fondly at Katie. "You're right, but a good lay isn't a bad place to start."

Pulling her feet down, Cid stood, dropped her cigarette in an ashtray, then faced the water. She was silent for a long while before finely turning and looking at Tally. "Do you think Mimi'd like San Francisco?"

"Yes," Tally said with a smile. "Yes, I think she would."

****

For the first time, Tally entered the vast room called Neptune's Spirit. Three forward walls were glass and allowed sunlight to spill across the rich hardwood floor. Cozy chairs and couches in shades of warm oranges and browns conveyed an air of intimacy and relaxed comfort. On the back wall, in the same colors, a simple and lovely swirled painting pulled the room together. In the center of the windowed path, a venerable pianist sat at a baby grand and softly played *I'm In The Mood For Love*.

Ready to conduct the ceremony, the cruise director stood just to the front of the piano, a stocky woman with a formidable smile that suggested she loved what she was doing.

The mysteries of the heart were wondrous, Tally thought, as she lifted Katie's hand to her lips.

Katie had never seemed lovelier; her thin strapped dress matched the color of the sunlight, her sable hair pulled softly back from her face and her blue eyes very serious, yet dancing with love.

There were close to a hundred couples in the room, for a moment Tally looked around smiling at the joy she saw, then she gazed at Katie and nothing else mattered.

The vows began.

"I come here today to speak of our love and commitment. We have intimate knowledge of each other gained through shared experiences, deep friendship and a covenant of trust.

I offer you all that I am and ever hope to be. I will hold myself true to you in thought and deed. I will love and honor the whole that is you. I will support your dreams and be your wind.

I offer you my heart to bind my promise to you, the promise to grow old loving you with passion, respect and tenderness."

Tally's hands gentle and confident, slowly opened a brown velvet box. She took Katie's hand in hers and carefully slipped a small, but brilliant pear-shaped emerald on her finger. "I love you."

Katie pressed her fingers to her eyes to hold back the tears. "Aye, Tally McGinnis, and I love you."

And then they kissed.

In the back corner of the large room, next to a huge white sheet cake, Cid leaned against the wall. Self-consciously she looked around and then quickly flicked a tear from her cheek.

"Now the commitment ceremony," Katie began as she and Tally strolled arm and arm along the deck, "is sadly not official, mind you, but it is a nice celebration of our love. And you know how we Irish enjoy a good party, Tally McGinnis. And then of course there's the honeymoon."

Tally looked at her with a loop-sided grin. "I already hung the "Do Not Disturb" sign on our cabin door."

Vincenzo Pallino suddenly rounded the corner nearly running into both Katie and Tally.

"Scusa, Scusa." His voice once again held the ring of authority.

"Telephone, my office," he said between exaggerated attempts at catching his breath. "Your mama, she insists on speaking with you." His thick hands hung in the air in a helpless gesture.

Tally gripped Katie's hand. "Has something happened?"

He shook his head. "She is, Signorina, how you say, very insistent. Beyond that she mentioned no tragedy. Capisce?"

In one quick motion, Tally and Katie headed for the stairwell.

****

"Tally darling, no need for you to say anything. I've only got a second, Marsha's waiting you know. I hated bothering you, but you did say you were going to call today and I so wanted to hear your voice...and of course I didn't want you worrying when you didn't find me home."

"Marsha?"

"Please don't interrupt, darling, you know how I hate impertinent behavior. Your friend, Marsha, has been such a dear. She found a fabulous auction in Sausalito and, if you can believe it, she even brought me a beautiful red rose when she arrived to pick me up. You have such thoughtful friends, darling."

Tally's hands began to shake. "No Mother!"

"It's a glorious, sunny day. Marsha asked me to tell you she's taking me by a place called Little Capitan on our way to Sausalito. She said I'd love the view."

"NO MOTHER, you can't go..."

"Must run, Darling Marsha said not to worry, she'll take good care of me. Tata and toodleoo."

"Call the police! She's a murderer! A serial killer!" Tally stared at the phone, static buzzing loudly. Slowly her terrified eyes met Katie's.

The End

Now available from Rising Tide Press:

<u>*By The Sea Shore*</u> *by Sandra A. Morris*

Sydney lurched to a halt at the kitchen door of '*The Shooting Gallery*'. She turned off the car and cradled her head on the steering wheel, seemingly in no hurry to leave the sanctuary of the BMW's compact interior. She chastised herself for following Jennifer when she left the airport. She had not been surprised that Jess Shore had been there. Harley had spoken with Meg the other day and knew that Jess and Buster were expected sometime that week. Just Sydney's luck that she had arrived when she did, running smack dab into Jennifer. Did Jennifer and Jess know each other, Sydney wondered. She couldn't imagine how, but one never knew.

To make things even worse, Jennifer had probably heard the honk of warning Sydney had been forced to blast when the dark figure had darted from the bushes outside Jess's place, directly into the path of her car. Had she not veered suddenly, she felt sure, she would have hit the stranger in black. She would call Jess later in the day and alert her to the incident. Strangers, especially this time of year, and dressed like some movie of the week cat burglar, were likely up to no good. Sydney knew that break-ins in the off-season were a problem for Provincetown's summer residents, and hoped that all was well at Jess's place.

Moving laboriously, Sydney crossed the narrow path to the door and entered the hub of the bistro, her home away from home: the kitchen.

The usually comforting sight of the gleaming copper pots and pans, the redolent smells of hundreds of spices and flavorings and the barren quiet of the interior beyond failed to ease the tension between her eyes.

"Damn you Jennifer Eastcott," she seethed aloud. Your timing sucks, she thought.

She swore an oath and whipped herself into a flurry of activity. Sydney didn't like discord and was determined to pull herself out of her current funk. Whatever the special was tonight, it would surely be chopped, pureed, or diced to within an inch of its life.

Sydney showed no mercy, even as she cleaved into an innocent carrot, sending half of it across the floor only to stop dead against a sneakered foot. She squinted at the silhouette in the doorway, recognition dawning sickly on her.

"What are you doing here?" Sydney questioned.

"I have a message for you, Sydney," the voice whispered.

From behind her, too late, Sydney sensed the presence of another body. As she turned, a white-hot pain exploded across the back of her head and all went dark...

More Fiction to Stir the Imagination
From Rising Tide Press

CLOUD NINE AFFAIR $11.99
Katherine E. Kreuter
Christine Grandy – rebellious, wealthy, twenty-something – has disappeared, along with her lover Monica Ward. Desperate to bring her home, Christine's millionaire father hires Paige Taylor. But the trail to Christine is mined with obstacles, while powerful enemies plot to eliminate her. Eventually, Paige discovers that this mission is far more dangerous than she dreamed. A witty, sophisticated mystery by the best-selling author of *Fool Me Once*, filled with colorful characters, plot twists, and romance.

STORM RISING $12.00
Linda Kay Silva
The excitement continues in this wonderful continuation of *TROPICAL STORM*. Join Megan and Connie as they set out to find Delta and bring her home. The meaning of friendship and love Is explored as Delta, Connie, Megan and friends struggle to stay alive and stop General Zahn. Again the Costa Rican Rain Forest is the setting for another fast-paced action adventure. Storm fans won't want to miss this next installment in the Delta Stevens Mystery Series.

TROPICAL STORM $11.99
Linda Kay Silva
Another winning, action-packed adventure featuring smart and sassy heroines, an exotic jungle setting, and a plot with more twists and turns than a coiled cobra. Megan has disappeared into the Costa Rican rain forest and it's up to Delta and Connie to find her. Can they reach Megan before it's too late? Will Storm risk everything to save the woman she loves? Fast-paced, full of wonderful characters and surprises. Not to be missed.

CALLED TO KILL $12.00
Joan Albarella
Nikki Barnes, Reverend, teacher and Vietnam Vet is once again entangled in a complex web of murder and drugs when her past collides with the present. Set in the rainy spring of Buffalo, Dr. Ginni Clayton and her friend Magpie add spice and romance as Nikki tries to solve the mystery that puts her own life in danger. A fun and exciting read.

AGENDA FOR MURDER $11.99
Joan Albarella
A compelling mystery about the legacies of love and war, set on a sleepy college campus. Though haunted by memories of her tour of duty in Vietnam, Nikki Barnes is finally putting back the pieces of her life, only to collide with murder and betrayal.

ONE SUMMER NIGHT $12.00
Gerri Hill
Johanna Marshall doesn't usually fall into bed with someone she just met, but Kelly Sambino isn't just anyone. Hurt by love and labeled a womanizer, can these two women learn to trust one another and let love find its way?

BY THE SEA SHORE $12.00
Sandra Morris   avail 10/00
A quiet retreat turns into more investigative work for Jess Shore in the summer town of Provincetown, MA. This page-turner mystery will keep you entertained as Jess struggles with her individuality while solving an attempted murder case.

AND LOVE CAME CALLING $11.99
Beverly Shearer
A beautifully told love story as old as time, steeped in the atmosphere of the Old West. Danger lights the fire of passion between two women whose lives become entwined when Kendra (Kenny), on the run from the law, happily stumbles upon the solitary cabin where Sophie has been hiding from her own past. Together, they learn that love can overcome all obstacles.

SIDE DISH $11.99
 Kim Taylor
A genuinely funny yet tender novel which follows the escapades of Muriel, a twenty-something burmed – out waitress with a college degree, who has turned gay slacker living into an art form. Getting by on margaritas and old movies, she seems to have resigned herself to low standards, simple pleasures, and erotic daydreams. But in secret, Muriel is searching for true love.

COMING ATTRACTIONS $11.99
Bobbi D. Marolt
Helen Townsend reluctantly admits she's tried of being lonely...and of being closeted. Enter Princess Charming in the form of Cory Chamberlain, a gifted concert pianist. And Helen embraces joy once again. But can two women find happiness when one yearns to break out of the closet and breathe free, while the other fears that it will destroy her career? A delicious blend of humor, heart and passion – a novel that captures the bliss and blundering of love.

ROUGH JUSTICE $10.99
Claire Youmans
When Glenn Lowry's sunken fishing boat turns up four years after its
disappearance, foul play is suspected. Classy, ambitious Prosecutor
Janet Schilling immediately launches a murder investigation, which
produces several surprising suspects-one of them, her own former lover
Catherine Adams, now living a reclusive life on an island. A real page-
turner!

NO CORPSE $12.00
Nancy Sanra
The third Tally McGinnis mystery is set aboard an Olivia Cruise. Tally
and Katie thought they were headed out for some sun and fun. Instead,
Tally finds herself drawn into a reunion cruise gone awry. When women
start turning up dead, it is up to Tally and Cid to find the murderer and
unravel a decades old mystery. Sanra fans new and old, won't be
disappointed.

NO ESCAPE $11.99
Nancy Sanra
This edgy, fast-paced whodunit set in picturesque San Francisco, will
keep you guessing. Lesbian PI Tally McGinnis is called into action
when Dr. Rebecca Toliver is charged with the murder of her lover
Melinda. Is the red rose left at the scene the crime the signature of a
copycat killer, or is the infamous Marcia Cox back, and up to her old,
evil tricks again?

NO WITNESSES $9.99
Nancy Sanra
This cliffhanger of a mystery set in San Francisco, introduces Detective
Tally McGinnis, whose ex-lover Pamela Tresdale is arrested for the
grisly murder of a wealthy Texas heiress. Tally rushes to the rescue
despite friends' warnings, and is drawn once again into Pamela's web of
deception and betrayal as she attempts to clear her and find the real
killer.

DEADLY RENDEZVOUS $9.99
Diane Davidson
A string of brutal murders in the middle of the desert plunges Lt. Toni
Underwood and her lover Megan into a high profile investigation, which
uncovers a world of drugs, corruption and murder, as well as the dark
side of the human mind. Explosive, fast-paced, & action-packed.

DEADLY GAMBLE $11.99
Diane Davidson
Las-Vegas-city of bright lights and dark secrets-is the perfect setting for
this intriguing sequel to *DEADLY RENDEZVOUS*. Former police
detective Toni Underwood and her partner Sally Murphy are catapulted
back into the world of crime by a letter from Toni's favorite aunt. Now a
prominent madam, Vera Valentine fears she is about to me murdered-a
distinct possibility.

RETURN TO ISIS $9.99
Jean Stewart
It is the year 2093, and Whit, a bold woman warrior from an Amazon
nation, rescues Amelia from a dismal world where females are either
breeders or drones. During their arduous journey back to the shining
all-women's world of Artemis, they are unexpectedly drawn to each
other. This engaging first book in the series has it all-romance, mystery,
and adventure.

ISIS RISING $11.99
Jean Stewart
In this stirring romantic fantasy, the familiar cast of lovable characters
begins to rebuild the colony of Isis, burned to the ground ten years
earlier by the dread Regulators. But evil forces threaten to destroy their
dream. A swashbuckling futuristic adventure and an endearing love
story all rolled into one.

WARRIORS OF ISIS $11.99
Jean Stewart
The third lusty tale is one of high adventure and passionate romance
among the Freeland Warriors. Arinna Sojourner, the evil product of
genetic engineering, vows to destroy the fledgling colony of Isis with her
incredible psychic powers. Whit, Kali, and other warriors battle to save
their world, in this novel bursting with life, love, heroines and villains.
A Lambda Literary Award Finalist

EMERALD CITY BLUES $11.99
Jean Stewart
When comfortable yuppie world of Chris Olson and Jennifer Hart
collides with the desperate lives of Reb and Flynn, two lesbian
runaways struggling to survive on the streets of Seattle, the forecast is
trouble. A gritty, enormously readable novel of contemporary lesbigay
life, which raises real questions about the meaning of family and
community. This book is an excellent choice for young adults and the
more mature reader.

DANGER IN HIGH PLACES $9.99
Sharon Gilligan
Set against the backdrop of Washington, D.C., this riveting mystery introduces freelance photographer and amateur sleuth, Alix Nicholson. Alix stumbles on a deadly scheme, and with the help of a lesbian congressional aide, unravels the mystery.

DANGER! CROSS CURRENTS $9.99
Sharon Gilligan
The exciting sequel to *Danger in High Places* brings freelance photographer Alix Nicholson face-to-face with an old love and a murder. When Alix's landlady turns up dead, and her much younger lover, Leah Claire, the prime suspect, Alix launches a frantic campaign to find the real killer.

HEARTSONE AND SABER $10.99
Jacqui Singleton
You can almost hear the sabers clash in this rousing tale of good and evil, of passionate love between a bold warrior queen and a beautiful healer with magical powers.

PLAYING FOR KEEPS $10.99
Stevie Rios
In this sparkling tale of love and adventure, Lindsay West an oboist, travels to Caracas, where she meets three people who change her life forever: Rob Heron a gay man, who becomes her dearest friend; her lover Mercedes Luego, a lovely cellist, who takes Lindsay on a life-altering adventure down the Amazon; and the mysterious jungle-dwelling woman Arminta, who touches their souls.

LOVESPELL $9.95
Karen Williams
A deliciously erotic and humorous love story in which Kate Gallagher, a shy veterinarian, and Allegra, who has magic at her fingertips, fall in love. A masterful blend of fantasy and reality, this beautifully written story will delight your heart and imagination.

NIGHTSHADE $11.99
Karen Williams
Alex Spherris finds herself the new owner of a magical bell, which some people would kill for. She is ushered into a strange & wonderful world and meets Orielle, who melts her frozen heart. A heartwarming romance spun in the best tradition of storytelling.

FEATHERING YOUR NEST: An Interactive Workbook& Guide to a
Loving Lesbian Relationship
Gwen Leonhard, M.ED./Jennie Mast, MSW $14.99
This fresh, insightful guide and workbook for lesbian couples provides
effective ways to build and nourish your relationships. Includes fun
exercises & creative ways to spark romance, solve conflict, fight fair,
conquer boredom, spice up your sex lives.

SHADOWS AFTER DARK $9.95
Ouida Crozier
While wings of death are spreading over her own world, Kyril is sent to
earth to find the cure. Here, she meets the beautiful but lonely Kathryn,
and they fall deeply in love. But gradually, Kathryn learns that her
exotic new lover has been sent to earth with a purpose – to save her
own dying *vampire* world. A tender, finely written story.

SWEET BITTER LOVE $10.99
Rita Schiano
Susan Fredrickson is a woman of fire and ice – a successful high-
powered executive, she is by turns sexy and aloof. From the moment
writer Jenny Ceretti spots her at the Village Coffeehouse, her serene life
begins to change. As their friendship explodes into a blazing love affair,
Jenny discovers that all is not as it appears, while Susan is haunted by
ghosts from a past that won't stay hidden. A roller-coaster romance
which vividly captures the rhythm and feel of love's sometimes rocky
ride and the beauty of life after recovery.

HOW TO ORDER

Please send me the books I have checked. I enclosed a check or money order, plus $4
for the first book and $1 for each additional book to cover shipping and handling.

NAME (Please Print) _____

ADDRESS _____

CITY _____ STATE _____ ZIP _____

Arizona residents please add 7% sales tax to total.

Send to: Rising Tide Press 3831 N. Oracle Rd. Tucson, Arizona 85705
Or visit our website: www.risingtidepress.com